THE GIFT OF THE MARQUESS

USA TODAY
BESTSELLING AUTHOR

DARCY BURKE

For Banana Cat
for giving all the snuggles

THE GIFT OF THE MARQUESS

The Marchioness of Darlington wants nothing more than a houseful of children, but after three years of marriage Poppy has given up hope. When she learns her husband doesn't share her sense of loss, Poppy tries to soothe her aching heart by helping at a local institution for single women and mothers. But the arrival of an expectant mother only reignites her longing, driving the wedge between her and Gabriel deeper.

After losing his mother and sister in childbirth, Gabriel, the Marquess of Darlington, is secretly glad his wife hasn't been able to conceive. He can't bear the thought of losing her, not even to achieve their dream of having a family. Desperate to prove his love, Gabriel makes a shocking proposition. It's a risk, but if he can overcome Poppy's fears and hesitation, he can give her what she wants most for Christmas.

Don't miss the rest of Love is All Around, a Regency Holiday Trilogy!

Book one: The Red Hot Earl

Book two: The Gift of the Marquess
Book three: Joy to the Duke

Love romance? Have a free book (or two or three) on me!

Sign up at http://www.darcyburke.com/readerclub for members-only exclusives, including advance notice of pre-orders and insider scoop, as well as contests, giveaways, freebies, and 99 cent deals!

Want to share your love of my books with like-minded readers? Want to hang with me and get inside scoop? Then don't miss my exclusive Facebook groups!

Darcy's Duchesses for historical readers
Burke's Book Lovers for contemporary readers

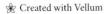

CHAPTER 1

County Durham, England
November 1811

A child's squeal rent the air, making Gabriel
Kirkwood, Marquess of Darlington, pause
in his hammering. Two small boys ran toward the
open doorway where Gabriel was repairing the
broken hinge. They stopped short, the taller boy
ramming into the shorter one, whom he was
chasing.

"Beggin' your pardon, my lord," the younger
boy, named Matthew, said, looking up at Gabriel
with wide blue eyes.

"Careful there," Gabriel said with a smile as he
glanced down the corridor over their heads. "Don't
let Mrs. Armstrong catch you running inside." The
overseer of the Institution for Impoverished
Women, which everyone referred to as Hartwell
House, expected order and discipline.

Matthew looked over his shoulder while his
older brother John shook his head. "We're careful,

my lord. She's busy," he added, as if to prove their diligence.

"Good." Gabriel went back to his work and finished hammering the new hinge into place.

"What're you doin'?" Matthew came up beside him, his curious gaze riveted on Gabriel's repair.

"I replaced the hinge so this door will close properly." Gabriel stood back. Hartwell House had been converted into the institution some fifteen years ago when the owner and his wife, the Armstrongs, had started taking in impoverished women, many with small children and no way to feed them. The only alternative for most of them was a workhouse, and that was no place to raise children, not if you wanted to spend time with them. Hartwell House allowed mothers and children to stay together, to build a life—together. "Go on, give it a try and see if I did a good job."

The boy shot him a dubious glance, and Gabriel nodded in encouragement. The lad swung the door closed, slamming it in his brother's face.

Giggling, Matthew put his hand over his mouth.

Gabriel kept himself from laughing. "Looks like it works fine."

The door pushed open to reveal the glaring eyes of John. "You didn't have to shut it in my face."

"I didn't mean to." Matthew looked up at Gabriel. "I'm glad you fixed it. It was too loud in here the other night." He made a face, then walked out of the room, which was the women-only dormitory.

Gabriel looked to John. "Why was it too loud?"

"Cryin', because someone died." John made the statement without a shred of sadness, which pulled at Gabriel's heart. What sort of tragedy had this boy already endured to be so unmoved by death?

Or, perhaps more accurately, the perspective of mortality had not yet visited the child. It wasn't until Gabriel was ten and he lost his mother that the unmanageable grief of death had forever altered his view. Life was precious and could change —or be gone—in a moment.

"I'm sorry to hear that," Gabriel said softly.

"There you are." Mrs. Armstrong's lilting voice carried down the corridor. "You boys are late for your midday meal. Get on with you, then." She arrived at the dormitory and gave them a warm but firm stare.

They didn't spare a parting glance for Gabriel, telling him just who held the higher rank here at Hartwell House—and it wasn't a marquess. Suppressing a smile, Gabriel turned to the formidable woman who ran the institution. Tall, with brown hair that was beginning to gray at the temples and a thin mouth that might have been cruel if she didn't laugh so much, Mrs. Armstrong was the heart of this place, especially since her husband had passed away the year before.

"I hope they weren't bothering you," she said, eyeing the door.

"Not at all. They were helping, in fact. It occurs to me that I could teach them some useful skills. If you think they're old enough."

"I do, and that would be wonderful." She beamed at him. "You and the marchioness are so lovely with all that you do for us here. I've been meaning to ask—and I hope you don't think me too forward—if her ladyship is all right. We haven't seen her in nearly a fortnight."

"Has it been that long?" Gabriel realized she hadn't come with him the last few times but hadn't counted the days. He read the concern in Mrs. Armstrong's eyes and sought to put her at ease.

"Poppy is fine, thank you. Just busy with things at home." Gabriel didn't know if that was true. He'd find out—Mrs. Armstrong's worry was now his.

"I'm glad to hear it," she said. "The children miss her."

A sharp pang sliced briefly through Gabriel's chest. Of course they did. Poppy spent most of her time here with the children, reading to them, playing with them, teaching them while their mothers sewed or worked in the garden. Hartwell House provided opportunities for the residents to work and earn money in the hope that they would eventually be able to leave and have their own household. Since he and Poppy didn't have children of their own, she enjoyed spending time with the youngest residents. She would have been a wonderful mother, but after nearly three years of marriage and no pregnancy, it seemed that was not to be.

Gabriel shook the thought from his head. "I heard someone died." He hoped the boy was mistaken, but the dark shadow that fell across Mrs. Armstrong's eyes told him he wasn't.

"So sad, but not surprising, unfortunately. The girl was so undernourished. Not really a girl, I suppose." Mrs. Armstrong shook her head, then frowned. "No, she *was* a girl who'd been about to become a mother."

Gabriel's breath stuck in his lungs as a tremor of dread snaked through him. *Oh no…*

He recalled the young woman—the girl—who'd arrived several weeks ago. She'd been nearly starving, and Mrs. Armstrong had done all she could to help her. "The babe?" Gabriel asked.

"Stillborn. The mother fell into an exhausted sleep and never woke up." She glanced toward one of the beds. "Already filled her space, though."

It was hard to think of that as a bright spot, but what else could the woman do? This was her life—assisting those she could and letting go those she couldn't.

Gabriel couldn't help but think of his wife, of his beloved Poppy, and their inability to have children. And how bloody *grateful* he was for that. For knowing he'd never lose her the way that poor girl had died. Or the way his mother had died. Or his older sister. Or Poppy's mother. All around him, women died in childbirth, and he had every expectation the same would happen to Poppy.

He couldn't bear the thought of it.

"Mrs. Armstrong?" A young woman named Judith who had worked for Mrs. Armstrong as long as Gabriel had been coming here stuck her head into the dormitory. "There's a new arrival."

"It never ends," Mrs. Armstrong said with a shake of her head. She started to turn, but hesitated. "I hope you don't think me impertinent, but if her ladyship is having trouble because of her condition, I'd be happy to talk with her about it."

Gabriel blinked at her, not certain what she meant. "Condition?"

"That she doesn't have children of her own." Mrs. Armstrong's voice was soft, her forehead creased with empathy. "You've been married, what, three years now?"

"Almost."

"That's right around the time I realized Mr. Armstrong and I weren't going to be blessed with children. The following year, we took in our first young woman. Helping her and her young son gave us joy and…purpose."

A small knot formed at the base of Gabriel's throat. He swallowed to keep it from rising. "I believe that's how Poppy feels about coming here—it brings her joy." And probably purpose. He wasn't sure.

Mrs. Armstrong's mouth bloomed into a caring smile. "That's good to hear. I hope she'll come back when she's ready. Now, if you'll excuse me."

"Of course," Gabriel murmured.

Alone once more, Gabriel cleaned up his tools and left the dormitory. He'd done all he could today, but there were always things to be done. The building was in sore need of rehabilitation. The roof might not even last the winter.

"You have to let me stay!" A woman's voice carried from the back corner where Mrs. Armstrong's office was located.

"I'm afraid we don't have accommodation for someone in your condition," Mrs. Armstrong said. "You're too ill. I'm so sorry. There is a workhouse—"

"No!"

The sound of coughing filled the air followed by a thump, as if someone had fallen.

"Good heavens!" Mrs. Armstrong declared, prompting Gabriel to stride toward the noise. Arriving at the office, he saw a crumpled form on the floor. Mrs. Armstrong and Judith knelt beside a woman whose coughs faded into a groan.

"Why didn't you say you were with child?" Mrs. Armstrong asked, aghast.

The woman on the floor answered with a cough.

"Can I offer assistance?" Gabriel asked.

Mrs. Armstrong looked up, relief flashing in her eyes. "Yes, thank you. Can you help us lift her to a chair?"

Gabriel moved farther into the office and looked down at the pale, unkempt woman. Her blonde hair was falling from its pins, and she wore a ratty cloak that opened to expose her clothing, which was dirty and torn. It also didn't fit well, stretching taut over her round belly.

He squatted down and gently lifted her to a sitting position between Mrs. Armstrong and the other woman.

"Let's get you to the chair," Mrs. Armstrong said.

"Why?" The woman tried to shrug her helpers away. "I need to find another place to stay."

Mrs. Armstrong looked at her with kind determination. "We'll make room. I'll give you my bed. You're not well, and you need to take care of yourself for the sake of the babe."

"I don't even want the brat," the woman said, scowling.

Mrs. Armstrong gave her a serene smile. "You might think that right now, but once you meet the babe, you'll change your mind."

She shook her head vehemently. Then promptly dissolved into a coughing fit. "I'll find someplace else," she rasped between coughs.

Mrs. Armstrong frowned. "You should stay here."

Controlling her cough, the woman looked at Gabriel. "Help me up, please?"

Gabriel put his arm around her and lifted her to stand. "I have an empty cottage on my estate. Would you like to stay there until you're well?"

Rising, Mrs. Armstrong looked at him in surprise. "She can't be alone. She needs care."

"You can't give up your bed, Mrs. Armstrong," Gabriel said. "I have an empty cottage."

"I'll go to care for her," Judith offered.

Mrs. Armstrong took a deep breath. "That's very kind of you, Judith. I shall miss you here, but of course you must go. If the woman is set on leaving, and if she'll have you." She sent an expectant look toward the pregnant woman.

"I am and I will." She sniffed loudly, a horrible sound that nearly made Gabriel cringe. "Where is this cottage?"

"I can take you there now," Gabriel said, glad he'd brought his cart today instead of riding his horse. It was difficult to deliver several sacks of flour on horseback.

"All right." The woman began coughing again, bending at the waist as she fought to stop.

"You'll need medicine," Mrs. Armstrong said to Judith. "And clothing for her that will fit properly."

Judith nodded. "I'll go see what I can find." She turned to leave.

"I'll pack a basket." Mrs. Armstrong pivoted toward Gabriel. "You'll have food and other necessities for them?"

"Of course." The cottage he had in mind had been vacant since last spring, but a neighbor had kept it clean and in good repair until a new tenant came along. He'd make sure to stock food and linens for them. Plus, he'd ask his steward to have the same neighbor look in on them. Not that Gabriel wouldn't also check on them regularly. He was keenly interested in the woman and the fact that she didn't want her baby.

A dream rooted in his mind… A dream he dared not hope for, and yet couldn't keep from wanting.

Mrs. Armstrong guided the woman to a chair. "What's your name, love?"

"Dinah Kitson."

"Come, Dinah, sit until it's time to go." Mrs. Armstrong made sure she was comfortable.

Dinah lifted her rheumy eyes to Gabriel. "Why are you helping me?"

"Because you're in need of help."

"What about the babe?" Dinah rested her hand on her belly.

"We'll sort that out," Gabriel said, cautioning himself to go slow. The woman was sick, and there was no telling what would happen—whether the babe would even survive. And Dinah could very well change her mind after it was born. She'd see its face and count its fingers and toes, and she'd fall hopelessly in love.

Yes, he had a dream, but he didn't really expect it to come true.

CHAPTER 2

*P*oppy Kirkwood, Marchioness of Darlington, sat before the fire in the sitting room adjacent to the bedchamber she shared with her husband. Her hand moved with quick precision, filling in the pattern of greenery on her needlepoint.

The piece was large and would look lovely hanging in the drawing room during Christmastime. Provided she finished it in time.

Gabriel came in after staying in the dining room to share port with his steward, who'd taken dinner with them. Charlie's wife was at home with their young children. The hollow ache that seemed to always reside in Poppy's chest sharpened briefly before she shrugged the sensation away.

"What are you working on?" Gabriel asked as he moved to sit beside her on the settee.

She spread it out across her lap as best she could so he could see it. "It's a wall hanging for the drawing room."

Gabriel angled himself toward her and surveyed the needlepoint. "Is that mistletoe?"

A smile teased her lips. "It is."

He pressed a quick kiss to her mouth. "I don't think it matters that it isn't real."

"Or hanging over us, apparently," she said wryly.

Grinning, he returned his attention to the hanging. "It's lovely. You've quite a hand for embroidery. Didn't you make a tablecloth for Hartwell House recently?"

Poppy stiffened. "A couple of months ago, yes."

"I was there today, as you know," he said, lifting his gaze to hers. "Mrs. Armstrong asked if you were all right. She's missed seeing you there."

Poppy carefully folded the needlework and set it aside as unease curled through her. "I've been busy."

"That's what I told Mrs. Armstrong. However, when I try to think of what you've been busy with, I'm afraid I don't know what could be keeping you from Hartwell House."

"You are occupied with your own endeavors." Indeed, it seemed he was more consumed than ever with estate matters—and with helping at Hartwell House. He enjoyed building and fixing things. When he wasn't in his workshop here, he was at the institution repairing something or other.

"I miss going there together," he said, reaching for her hands, which she'd folded in her lap after moving the needlework. "Perhaps you'd like to go with me tomorrow or the next day?" His lips curved into a soft smile that was so at odds with the square set of his chin and the chiseled line of his jaw and cheekbones. It was that smile that had claimed her attention three years ago at a local assembly. But his humor and concern for others had won her heart.

Straightening her spine, she answered, "I'm afraid I won't be able to."

His smile dipped, turning to a slight frown. "Is there something amiss? Some reason you don't want to visit Hartwell House anymore?"

The concern in his eyes unraveled her closely held composure. She stood from the settee, nervous energy spiraling through her. "No." She stepped toward the hearth, her suddenly cold body seeking the heat of the fire.

He rose behind her—she could feel his presence as he moved close. "I wondered if perhaps...if it bothered you to spend time with the children there?"

She turned toward him, surprised by the accuracy of his query. "Is that what you think?"

He lifted a shoulder. "Mrs. Armstrong mentioned it. She's happy to speak with you—to lend support—if you wish."

"You discussed our problems with her?" Poppy liked Mrs. Armstrong very much, but this wasn't something one talked about with those outside the family. In Poppy's case, it wasn't something she talked about ever.

"She brought it up. She's concerned about you." His brow creased. "As am I."

Emotion bubbled inside her—sadness and frustration—but she refused to surrender to despair. She'd cried too many tears. "I don't want your pity. I don't want anyone's pity, not even my own. I am trying to find a way to accept that this is what my life will be, and I can't do that with children running about. You seem to have no problem being there." She tried to keep the irritation from her tone, but feared she failed. "How have you accepted our fate?"

He blinked, then glanced toward the fire. When

his gaze met hers once more, she saw something odd, something she'd never seen before. "I will admit it wasn't as difficult for me as it seems to be for you."

Poppy's jaw nearly dropped to the floor. She felt as if all the air in her lungs had been squeezed out and that it might never return.

He continued, "While I would have liked to be a father, I can't say I'm sorry you won't suffer the risks of pregnancy and childbirth."

Now she knew what was in his eyes—relief. He was glad they hadn't conceived. He hadn't accepted anything. He'd welcomed their lot while she wallowed in sadness and disappointment.

"You're *happy*?" the question came out small and so soft, she wondered if he even heard her, because it took him a moment to respond.

"Not happy, no. But it's not the end of the world to me."

The end of the world... "That's a bit hyperbolic." She tried to make sense of what he was saying. He'd never revealed this to her before, and she almost felt...betrayed. "You don't understand how I am affected."

"Of course I do," he said, the furrows in his brow deepening while his eyes narrowed. "But perhaps you don't comprehend how *I* feel."

"Oh, I think I do." He had the blessing of feeling *relieved* while she suffered. And here she thought he'd suffered too.

He edged toward her, his height making him tower above her. "Do you? Do you know the anguish I feel when I hear of another soul lost to childbirth? Just today, Mrs. Armstrong told me of a girl—a *girl*—who died along with her stillborn babe."

She insulated herself to the pain in his tone. It

was nothing when compared with her torment. "Yes, it's tragic, but it's also life."

"And death. I don't want to lose you the way you lost your mother, the way I lost my mother and sister."

She notched her chin up, bothered that he would mention *her* mother, whom she'd lost at the age of two when her mother had given birth to Poppy's younger sister and whom she didn't even remember. Her memories were all things she'd been told by their father and by their older brother, Calder. She was also sensitive to how deeply Gabriel grieved the loss of his own mother when he was young. "You can't go through life fearing death. It awaits us all."

Anger flashed in his eyes. "I know that. But not yet. Not *now*."

She wanted him to understand her sorrow. "I'd risk it. Don't you want to leave something of us behind? If you fear death, think of how children, how a family makes us immortal."

He stared at her, his jaw working as his teeth clenched and unclenched. "I've lost too many people, and losing you would be a living death."

The ache inside her leapt, hungry for a kindred soul. "You've described precisely how I feel. Empty. Cold. Alone."

His pulse beat in his throat. He lifted his hand and cupped her cheek. "How can you feel alone with me? Am I—is my love—not enough?"

It wasn't. And yet it was. Mostly. Maybe. She didn't know. All she knew was that she needed to banish this heartache.

She brought her hands up and gripped the lapels of his jacket. "Make it enough. Make it *everything*."

Gabriel stared into her eyes as expectation

grew between them. She feared he would walk away.

He didn't.

He thrust his hand back into her hair, dislodging pins as he cupped her scalp. Then his lips devoured hers in a searing kiss.

She tightened her hands on his coat, holding him against her as she thrust her tongue into his mouth, claiming everything he would give her. Wrapping his other arm around her hips, he drew her to his body, pressing her pelvis to his.

Desperate need sparked within her. This was unlike anything she'd ever experienced. She wanted this—*him*—to take her away from the pain in her heart. Casting thought aside, she gave all her attention to him, to the storm gathering between them.

Anger and hurt and desire swirled together as she pushed at his coat, eager to strip him bare and lose herself in the only thing that would make her feel whole. Maybe not whole, but not completely hollow either.

Gabriel pulled at her hair, freeing the tresses until she felt them cascade down her back. Then he helped her get his coat off, discarding it to the floor. She flicked at the buttons of his waistcoat, and that garment quickly followed the first. With a grunt, he picked her up and carried her the short distance to their bedchamber. There, he set her down beside the bed and began undressing her, his movements quick and efficient.

Ruthless.

He tossed her shoes away and spun her around to pluck at the laces of her gown. In a trice, the garment pooled at her feet. He pushed her petticoat down over her body to join it.

His lips and tongue rained pleasure on the back

of her neck as he loosened her corset. A moment later, it fell from her as the rest had done, leaving her clad in her chemise and stockings. He kissed along the back of her shoulder, his teeth gently scoring her flesh while his hands came around and cupped her breasts through the cotton of her undergarment.

She gasped at the roughness of his touch, his thumbs and fingers drawing on her nipples. Raw lust shot straight to her sex. She wanted him now.

"Gabriel, I need you."

"You'll have me." He pulled her chemise up, baring her backside. "Bend."

She did as he instructed, bracing her hands on the bed in front of her as she bowed at the waist. One hand moved between her thighs while the other dove beneath her chemise, rending it slightly at the front, to further torment her breast. He cupped and squeezed, teasing more sensation from her than he ever had before.

He stroked her sex, and she arched back, seeking more of his touch. He slid his finger into her, filling her. She closed her eyes and curled her fingers into the coverlet.

He kissed the side of her neck, then nipped her earlobe. "Do you feel empty now?" He thrust up into her, and she pressed forward, rubbing her clitoris against the bed.

"No." She gasped as ecstasy curled inside her.

"Good." He put two fingers in her, pumping in and out, driving her toward a mad climax.

She clutched at the bed and snapped her hips back and forth with his rhythm. His hand left her breast, moving down between her and the mattress to flick her clitoris, again and again, sending her over the top of the mountain as she came apart in his arms.

Without waiting to fully recover, she turned and pulled at the buttons of his breeches. As soon as they were unfastened, he bent to pull off his boots, grunting and swearing with the effort. Then he stripped the stockings from her legs while she whisked the chemise over her head and threw it aside.

Casting the rest of his clothing off with vocal impatience, he climbed into the bed, pushing her onto the mattress. He kissed her savagely, and she gloried in the heat and despair of their joining. No, she wouldn't think. She would only feel.

He moved down to her breasts, his lips and tongue blazing a path of stark rapture. She reached down between them and found his sex, curling her hand around the base of his cock. He groaned, and she squeezed, milking him as she tugged up and slid back down. His hips moved against her, and moisture slicked her hand.

He found her clitoris again, stroking wildly as he suckled her breast. She cried out as pleasure built within her once more.

"Fill me," she begged. "Now. Take away the emptiness."

He rose up and looked down at her. "You are never alone, not so long as I am here."

The anguish inside her split as he drove into her. She pulled him down on top of her, seeking his weight and the security he gave her—an anchor in this tumult. Moisture wetted her cheeks, and she prayed he didn't feel it or see it. She didn't want to think. She only wanted to feel.

And the feelings had taken over.

Yes, he filled her, but she knew nothing would come of it. Never mind the ecstasy flashing within her as he thrust toward her barren womb. Or the way her body responded by meeting him, her legs curling around him and drawing him deeper and deeper, as if this time would be different. As if the ferocity of their passion could change their fortune.

She knew it would not.

Still, she flew. Higher and higher until she stood at the precipice. Then he kissed her, bringing them together even more completely, filling her as she'd demanded.

The climax rushed over her, sending her falling into darkness. Only this time, she knew the darkness would win.

This time, she welcomed it.

CHAPTER 3

*T*ime was not Poppy's friend. She counted days and tracked her cycle, always aware of when her courses should start. And painfully disappointed when they did. It was a vicious game that she invariably lost, and she wondered what would happen if she stopped playing.

Maybe she would stop feeling disappointed. Maybe she would look to other aspects of her life besides her inability to have a child.

That was what she *should* do, but finding the strength, the courage, to do so was incredibly difficult. Particularly when she felt so alone.

Only she wasn't alone. Not really.

The parchment in her hands—a note from her sister Bianca—was proof of that. As was Gabriel. He'd told her last night that she would never be alone.

After he'd revealed that he did not share her sorrow regarding their childlessness.

Learning that had torn a hole in her heart. She'd always thought they were united in their desire to conceive, but all along, he'd been relieved she hadn't. Had he also been hopeful? It was a minor distinction, but it mattered. To her, anyway.

Setting aside the note from her sister, she stood from her desk in the sitting room outside her bedchamber and strolled to the window. The day was gray and nondescript, mirroring the way she felt inside.

One would think she would have felt better following their coupling last night. That had been an extraordinary experience—the physicality, the emotion. But in the end, the emptiness had remained. Now she wished he hadn't told her his true feelings. Sometimes ignorance was a far more desirable state.

Oh hell. She didn't want to be ignorant. Nor did she want to wallow in grief any longer. It was time —the word provoked a short, harsh laugh—to stop playing this unwinnable game. Time was precisely what she needed. Time to accept and move on.

Turning from the window, she strode from the sitting room in search of Gabriel. She found him downstairs in his study. The door was slightly ajar, but she knocked lightly anyway.

"Come in," Gabriel called. She pushed open the door and stepped inside. He smiled at her, his gaze dipping over her in warm appreciation. "You look lovely today."

She didn't return his smile, nor did she approach his desk. She wasn't ready to talk with him about last night and about putting this all behind them. *Time*, she reminded herself. "Thank you."

"I was hoping we might go for a ride later since the day is quite fair." It had rained the last few days.

"I'm afraid I already have plans." She didn't really. She was simply stealing time. "I came to tell you that I'll be attending Lord Thornaby's house party with my sister on Thursday."

Gabriel leaned back in his chair. He'd declined the invitation. He didn't care for Thornaby or his friends. "You're a kind sister to chaperone her. Why on earth does she even want to go?"

"A variety of reasons. She is, as you know, rather sociable. She is also, as you know, unmarried. That is a situation I'm sure my brother wishes to rectify as soon as possible."

Gabriel snorted. "Your brother is a toad."

"Sometimes, yes." Poppy exhaled. "He is still my brother."

"Chill is *always* a toad—or worse." Chill was the name he'd been called since childhood, for he'd been the Earl of Chilton until their father's death. "Since the moment I met him, before he inherited the title, he was a blackguard. His progression from careless rake to haughty churl was certainly interesting. How one can actually alter their character for the worst is beyond me. Especially someone with such lovely sisters. It's as if he was raised by different parents."

"In a way, he was," she said softly. She didn't disagree with Gabriel, but today she didn't want to agree with him either. "He had our mother for much longer than I did, while Bianca didn't have her at all. Calder wasn't always the way you describe him."

"That's what you say. It seems he keeps devolving. We can only speculate how unpleasant he'll be in another decade."

Irritation curled along Poppy's spine. She didn't want to listen to Gabriel insult her brother, even if Calder deserved it. "The house party lasts until Saturday." Aside from chaperoning Bianca, Poppy thought the time away from Gabriel might help. She might even decide to stay at Hartwood with Bianca for a few days.

He frowned. "Are you angry with me?"

Her tongue twisted as she searched for the right

answer. She wasn't sure she *had* an answer, right or otherwise. "I don't know what I am. I just need... time." She straightened, pushing her shoulders back. "I told you—I'm trying to accustom myself to disappointment."

He stood and started around the desk. "It doesn't have to be like that—"

She held up a hand, cutting him off. "Please don't. I'd rather not listen to you offer comfort. Clearly, our perspectives couldn't be more different."

Spinning on her heel, Poppy stalked from the study back up to the sitting room. She went to the desk and dashed off a response to Bianca saying she would accompany her to Thornaby's house party.

After folding the parchment, she stood to take it to a groom for delivery to Hartwood. While downstairs, perhaps she ought to apologize to Gabriel. He was trying to be supportive, even if he *was* relieved that her dreams wouldn't come true.

She flinched at the characterization. Yet it was precisely their situation.

This breach would take time to heal. Even so, she shouldn't snap at his efforts.

Taking the letter, she went back to his study to apologize. However, he wasn't there, so she went in search of the butler and asked if he knew where Gabriel had gone.

"For a ride, my lady," Walker answered. "He just left a few moments ago if you'd like to catch him."

"Thank you, Walker. Will you have this letter delivered to Hartwood, please?"

He nodded. "Right away."

Poppy quickly fetched her cloak, hat, and gloves before dashing out toward the stables. Almost immediately, she realized she should have changed into boots, but she didn't plan to be out long, and the stable wasn't far.

Hurrying along, she strode toward the stable and caught sight of Gabriel on foot up ahead. However, he altered course, veering right onto a path that led toward one of the roads on the estate.

Poppy followed him but didn't try to overtake him—he walked too quickly for her. She'd do her best to keep him in view and when he stopped, she'd join him.

They continued for quite some time, and she wondered why he was walking instead of riding. Had she ruined his plans by declining his offer?

He approached a cottage. Smoke curled from the chimney, and a woman stood outside. Poppy tried to recall who lived there but couldn't. In fact, if pressed, she would have insisted it was vacant.

Clearly, it wasn't.

Gabriel strode toward the woman, his movements full of purpose as he stopped before her. She lifted her face, and Poppy recognized her from Hartwell House. Mrs. Armstrong had taken her in as a girl.

Why was she at the cottage? And why was Gabriel going to see her? A knot of unease twined in Poppy's gut.

Judith laughed—a warm, gentle sound that carried to Poppy on the wind. Gabriel joined in. Jealousy knifed through Poppy's chest, and she told herself she was being ridiculous. But then he touched Judith's arm, and she turned, leading him into the cottage.

Poppy ought to go and confront them, but she was rooted to the ground. A dozen scenarios swirled in her mind, but she kept coming back to one—they were having an affair.

The roots came free, and Poppy walked toward

the cottage. With each step, the knot in her belly tightened.

When she reached the door, she froze, her resolve weakening. What was she going to do? If he *was* having an affair, this was going to be a very ugly—and awkward—confrontation. Did that mean she should walk away?

No, she was not going to endure one more thing. She lifted her hand and loudly rapped on the door.

A moment later, Gabriel answered, his eyes widening as he saw her standing outside. "Poppy?"

"What's going on here?" She hadn't meant to ask so forcefully or indelicately, but her patience was simply gone. Pushing through the doorway, she looked around the small main room. "Where is Judith?"

The young woman came from the back of the cottage. She tucked a strand of blonde hair behind her ear. "Lady Darlington!"

Gabriel and Judith glanced at each other, lending them an air of guilt or conspiracy. Poppy folded her hands over her chest. "Judith, why aren't you at Hartwell House?"

"I—"

Gabriel cut her off. "She's here taking care of a woman because there were no more beds at Hartwell House. Rather than allow Mrs. Armstrong to give up her bed, I insisted the woman come stay in the empty cottage. Furthermore, she is ill, and this way, she can't spread her sickness to anyone else."

"Except for Judith." Poppy pursed her lips at him. "And you, apparently."

"Who's there?" a feminine voice called from the back room. This was followed by a coughing fit. Whoever was there was truly ill. There was no af-

fair, then. Poppy felt foolish for even thinking it—
Gabriel wasn't that type of husband.

"My goodness," Poppy breathed, striding past
both Gabriel and Judith and making her way into
the single bedroom.

The woman in the bed struggled to sit, but
Poppy was frozen by the sight of her round belly.
Forcing herself to take a deep breath, Poppy went
to the bed. "Let me help you." She grasped the
woman's arm and slid her other hand behind her
back as she shimmied up against the headboard.

"Who are you?" The woman narrowed her eyes
at Poppy.

"This is Lady Darlington, my wife." Gabriel
came into the bedroom with Judith on his heels.
"Poppy, this is Dinah Kitson. As you can see, she is
expecting, as well as being sick. She went to
Hartwell House, but Mrs. Armstrong didn't have
room for her. I offered to let her stay here, and Judith volunteered to come and nurse her until the
babe comes."

Poppy turned her head toward him. "How
long has she been here, and why didn't you
tell me?"

His jaw tensed, and his gaze flicked toward the
bed. "Only since yesterday. You've been busy."

Except she hadn't been, not really, and he'd
called her on it last night. Which meant he'd kept
the information from her on purpose. Because
Dinah was pregnant.

She returned her attention to Dinah. "Perhaps
you should come stay in the house so I can look
after you. Then Judith can return to Hartwell
House, where she is needed." Poppy could only
imagine that Mrs. Armstrong was now short-
handed. And here Poppy had avoided going there.
She suddenly felt very selfish.

"What if she gets everyone in the household sick?" Gabriel had a point.

"Very well, but I can come stay here to care for her so Judith can return," Poppy offered.

Gabriel came forward and gently clasped her elbow, then guided her from the room. "Poppy, I don't want you to fall ill."

She pulled her arm from his grasp. "You can't protect me from everything. This woman needs help, and Mrs. Armstrong needs Judith."

"Mrs. Armstrong had no problem with Judith coming here. It won't be for very long anyway. Dinah is already showing improvement after taking medicine, and her time is likely near."

There was that word again.

His gaze was cool. "Since you're so concerned about Mrs. Armstrong, perhaps you should start visiting Hartwell House again."

"I plan to. After the house party. In the meantime, I'll make sure Dinah is well situated. The physician should come see her."

"He will be here tomorrow," Gabriel said, the muscles in his jaw working. He lowered his voice. "Poppy, I didn't want to expose you to her."

"Because she's sick?" Poppy asked innocently, knowing she was likely pricking his ire and unable to stop herself.

"You know why. You said so just a little while ago—you're trying to become accustomed to disappointment."

"Yes, I am. Oddly, I think helping Dinah—and returning to Hartwell House—is exactly what I need." Yes, devoting herself to others would make the time pass. And maybe time would cease to be her enemy.

"If you think so." He didn't sound convinced. But it wasn't up to him.

"I do. Now let me make sure our patient is comfortable. Then we must prepare for the babe."

The thought of having a baby to care for, if only for a little while, filled Poppy with joy. Gabriel's brow creased, and Poppy turned away from his worry. She went back to the bedroom, to the woman who had finally pulled Poppy from the pit of grief.

Poppy removed her hat and smiled at Dinah. "I'm so glad you came. Is there anything I can bring for you?"

$\approx$

*T*his was not going the way Gabriel had planned.

He stood in the corner of the room as Poppy talked with Dinah and Judith about fetching more blankets and pillows from the house.

"How about books?" Poppy asked.

Dinah looked suddenly...shy. That wasn't a word Gabriel would have thought to attribute to her. "I like books about nature if you have any of those. And maybe plays?"

Poppy nodded, then turned to Judith. "Before I go, why don't you tell me what I can bring to supplement the kitchen here? Food, cookware, whatever you need."

"Thank you, my lady." Judith listed a few items, and Poppy said she'd have them delivered before the end of the day.

A few minutes later, she and Gabriel departed. Gabriel felt as if he were being swept out on a whirlwind. It was thrilling to see Poppy so engaged, but also frustrating since he wasn't able to accomplish his goal of speaking to Dinah about the baby.

And he wasn't about to do it in front of Poppy. What if Dinah rejected his proposal out of hand? What if she accepted it and then changed her mind? *If* Dinah decided to give her baby to him and Poppy to raise, Gabriel wanted to be certain it happened. As certain as he could be, anyway.

As they walked from the cottage, Gabriel looked over at his wife. The lines of her face were incredibly delicate, from the arch of her cheekbones to the tilt of her nose, but the lush fullness of her lips anchored the whole. She appeared serene, her slate-blue eyes trained forward as dark curls grazed her temple. He marveled at how her beauty could still make his heart pause and then speed before taking flight.

But what was going on behind that beloved façade? Was she still upset with him? Based on her irritation in his study earlier, he'd assumed she was. Then she'd come to the door of the cottage and had seemed even angrier.

"How did you come to be at the cottage?" he asked.

"I followed you. I went to your study to apologize for snapping at you, but Walker said you'd gone for a ride." She slid him a quick look. "Clearly that was not the case." She still sounded annoyed.

"I changed my mind." He decided it was better to clear the air between them. "What were you thinking when you came to the cottage?"

"I was wondering why you would come here to meet Judith of all people. I also wondered why she wasn't at Hartwell House. Seeing the two of you together..." Her lips pressed together, and her jaw tightened.

They had just walked out onto the narrow road. He stopped and gently clasped her forearm, turning toward her. "You thought I was meeting her for an assignation?"

She pivoted, facing him, her brow creasing. "I didn't know what to think. And since you didn't tell me she was here—or about Dinah—I had to ask."

He let go of her arm. "I'm sorry I didn't tell you. I wanted to help Mrs. Armstrong. After last night and what you said, I worried Dinah's presence might upset you."

Her gaze held his for a long moment, her face tense. "I wish you'd told me straightaway, but I understand why you didn't."

Gabriel moved, lessening the distance between them. He cupped her face, tracing his thumb along her cheekbone. "I would never have an affair. You have to know there is no other woman anywhere who could take me from you."

Desire pulsed through him. He wanted to show her how true those words were, how deeply he wanted her. Needed her. Loved her. He lowered his mouth to hers, sliding his hand back to her nape and holding her firm as he kissed her.

Tension arced through him as he awaited her reaction… She didn't pull away. Her hands lightly clutched his waist, and she tipped her head to mold her lips to his.

Overcome, he deepened the kiss, sliding his tongue against hers. She met him eagerly, her fingers digging into his sides. He pressed forward, and she moved her hands back, pulling him against her. His cock rose, hardening. He wanted to make sure she knew…

He pulled his lips from hers and grabbed her hand. Without a word, he glanced about, then stalked the way they'd come toward a stand of trees that would offer at least a modicum of privacy.

When he veered from the road toward the trees, she stopped. "Where are we going?"

He inclined his head. "There."

She looked at him as if he were mad. "Why?"

He pulled her against him. "Because I want you to know that you are the only one for me. Now and forever." He kissed her again but wasn't gentle about it. He claimed her mouth, clashing lips and tongues and teeth.

She drew away with a gasp. "I am not wearing boots, and the ground—"

Kissing her again, he didn't need her to finish. He swept her into his arms and carried her behind the trees so they weren't openly visible to the road. She curled her arms around his neck as he surveyed the area. One of the trees had a large exposed root system.

He set her on the root with the tree at her back.

"You don't have to do this," she said.

He brought his hand up beneath her cloak and grazed his thumb across her breast. The nipple was impossible to feel beneath her clothing. He cupped her instead, squeezing gently. "I think I do. I want to banish any question you could ever have." He looked into her eyes. Her pupils were starting to dilate.

He bent his head and kissed her neck just beneath her ear. Licking along her flesh, he moved down her throat, then cursed her cloak. "You're mine, and I am yours." He nipped her and sucked, making her cry out.

Lifting his head, he stared at her with naked need. "Tell me to stop. If you want to."

She shook her head. Then she splayed her hand

against his neck and dragged her thumb over his mouth. "Don't stop."

He sucked the digit between his lips. She closed her eyes and moaned softly, her head falling back. With a low growl, he kissed her again, this time with a savage, desperate need. Her fingers curled into his flesh, and he wished she wasn't wearing gloves. Or anything else.

His gloves were going to be a bloody nuisance. He quickly stripped them away, then lifted the hem of her skirt. Grasping the layers of her clothing took effort, but he managed to bunch them up at her waist.

She gasped into his mouth, pulling back slightly. "Cold."

"I'll make you warm." He skimmed across her thigh and found her sex. God, she was so wet. As he sank his finger into her heat, he was glad he'd abandoned the gloves. Her hips moved, drawing him deeper as she clutched at his shoulders.

This was insanity, but he was past the point of rational thinking. "Hold your skirts," he rasped as he withdrew from her body and worked to unfasten his breeches.

She did as he asked. "Hurry." Compounding matters—in the best way—she lifted one leg and wrapped it around his hips.

He freed his cock and pressed himself to her sex. She let go of her dress and clasped his hip, pulling him forward. He thrust up into her, and her moan filled the air with erotic promise.

Grabbing her backside, he lifted her. "Wrap both your legs around me and don't let go."

Pinning her between his body and the wide trunk, he prayed this would work, that they wouldn't tumble to the ground in an ungainly tangle. But with the second thrust, he realized this wasn't going to last terribly long. Pleasure raced through him, and her muscles were already beginning to contract around him. Letting go, he drove into her as an overwhelming feeling of passion and possession seized him.

He stared into her enraptured face. "Look at me."

Her eyes came open, the gray blue a haze of seductive desire. "You are mine, and I am yours," he repeated. "Say it."

"You are mine, and I am yours."

He drove deep, hating her womb in that moment—or his cock, whatever was preventing her dream. Even if it was a dream that scared the hell out of him. "Now and forever."

She moved her hand to cup his face. "Now and forever." Her lids fluttered, and her long, dark lashes brushed her cheeks as she closed her eyes. "Preferably *now*."

Her muscles clenched around him fiercely, and her cries rent the air. He grunted, then cried out as he came apart inside her. They both held on as if the power of their climaxes would do what he feared and send them to the ground.

He buried his face in her neck, inhaling her sweet honeyed scent. She held him to her, her hands a powerful anchor for his trembling body.

Easing her down, he withdrew from her and drew deep breaths of air into his lungs. Her skirts fell between them, and she pressed back against the tree, taking deep breaths.

While he refastened his breeches, she turned from him and put herself to rights for a moment. When she faced him once more, she was again the serene beauty who'd left the cottage. His wild, ardent lover was gone.

Tension stretched between them, and he began to wonder if it would ever go away.

Guarded, he asked, "What's wrong? Are you still upset about Judith and Dinah?"

"Sexual gratification doesn't solve anything."

"I'd argue with that," he said, feeling supremely satisfied. He sobered. "I'm sorry I didn't tell you."

"Thank you." She pressed her lips together and sucked them in briefly before exhaling. "I need some time to adjust—to what you told me last night. Not having children has been—is—incredibly painful for me. To learn that it isn't for you, that you're content to remain childless is also painful. I need...time."

He offered a faint smile. "We have forever."

She didn't smile, but she didn't frown either. "Yes, we do."

He offered her his arm and was glad when she took it for the walk back to the house. "Content isn't the right word. It isn't that I don't want children, especially because I know what a wonderful mother you would be."

She stiffened, and he wished he hadn't said that. Actually, no, he didn't. It was the truth. And if he'd learned anything in recent days—and today—it was that he should always tell her the truth, even when it was painful.

They walked for several minutes in silence. He wondered what was going on in her mind. Was her melancholy taking hold again, or was she focused on Dinah? Perhaps he could help her do the latter despite the fact that he didn't particularly want her involved with the woman. On second thought, maybe it was for the best. Maybe Dinah would offer the babe to Poppy.

And perhaps *he* should focus on repairing the

rift between him and his wife. "How much time do you need?" he asked softly.

"I don't know. Let's talk again when I return from Thornhill."

Gabriel hated the uneven ground between them, but acknowledged that he alone couldn't make it smooth. He'd have to be patient. There was simply nothing else he could do.

CHAPTER 4

After Gabriel left the following day for Hartwell House, Poppy walked to the cottage. She carried a basket with biscuits from the cook and a play she hoped Dinah would like.

Though Judith had told her the day before that she needn't knock, Poppy did anyway. A moment later, Judith answered. "You don't have to—"

"Knock, I know. But I don't think I can break the habit. I brought biscuits from the cook." She handed Judith the basket as she stepped into the cottage.

"How lovely!" Judith peeked inside. "What else is there?"

"A play. I thought I might read to Dinah if she's amenable."

Judith's fair brows arched briefly. "She's a bit disagreeable since Dr. Fisk's visit earlier."

"Oh, he's already been?" Poppy had hoped to be here when he arrived.

Judith nodded. "He told her to rest as much as possible, so the play, whether she allows you to read it or not, will not come amiss. He also left some milk of sow thistle to help with her cough. I was just about to make some tea with it. I'll fix you a cup—without the sow thistle," she added with a grin.

"Thank you. I'll come back for the play if things go well." She winked at Judith before walking back to the bedroom. "Good afternoon, Dinah," she called in warning before stepping over the threshold.

Perched on the edge of the bed, Dinah, her dark blonde hair swept onto her head save a few strands that grazed the left side of her face, grunted in response.

"Are you going somewhere?" Poppy asked.

"Just to the chair. I can't stay in this bed all the time."

"Of course you can't. Do you need any help?"

Dinah silently glared her response, her dark brown eyes snapping. Poppy snagged her lower lip lest she say something, then turned to deposit her cloak and bonnet on a hook.

As she pivoted back, Dinah was just settling into the chair, lowering her small frame slowly so that she looked far older than her perhaps twenty years. Dinah angled her round belly toward the fireplace, which sat between this room and the main room where Judith was preparing the tea.

Poppy tugged her gloves off and tucked them into the pocket of her cloak. Since there was only the one chair, she went to the narrow bench that stood at the end of the bed and moved it closer to the fireplace so she could sit by Dinah.

"How are you feeling today?" Poppy asked conversationally.

"Fine."

"I brought biscuits, and Judith is making tea."

Dinah's eyes narrowed. "What kind of biscuits?"

"Lemon." A light sparked in Dinah's eyes. "Do you like lemon?" Poppy asked.

She blinked the gleam of interest away, and the stoic young woman returned. "Yes."

"You've had lemon biscuits before, I take it?"

"A few times."

Poppy had tried to glean information from Dinah about her background, particularly the circumstances that led to her condition. She wasn't married—that much she'd admitted. "Do you know how to make them?"

Dinah shook her head. "The cook said it wasn't hard." Her eyes widened briefly, and she turned her head to frown at the fire.

Judith came in with a small tray bearing their two cups of tea and a plate of biscuits. She looked about, clearly wondering where to set the items.

Poppy patted the empty space on the bench beside her. "Put the tray here. Thank you, Judith."

After depositing the refreshments, Judith departed. Poppy picked up the plate and offered it to Dinah with a smile. "Here you are."

Dinah tentatively took one, her eyes as wary as they'd ever been, as if she expected Poppy to snatch the confection back from her fingers. She took a bite, and her expression relaxed into a joy Poppy had never seen on her face before.

"I'll have Cook make another batch," Poppy said before taking one for herself and setting the plate back down.

"Yes, please," Dinah said before she had swallowed. "They're delicious."

"I'm glad you like them. The cook you mentioned—was that your cook?" Poppy didn't think that was the case but didn't want to make any assumptions.

Dinah laughed as she reached over the arm of the chair for another biscuit. "No, my mother did all the cooking when I was young. Until I went to work in the scullery in the—" She cut off whatever she was going to say by taking a bite.

Poppy picked up her tea. "You were a scullery maid?"

"For a few years." She continued to nibble at her biscuit.

"Did you like that?"

"Not particularly. I was relieved to be promoted to upstairs maid."

But then she'd become pregnant. Poppy wondered by whom and why the jackanapes hadn't married her. "Did you leave the position when you became pregnant?" she asked softly.

"In a manner of speaking." Her response was terse, her eyes blazing with fury.

"They let you go?" When Dinah glared at the fire, Poppy softly added, "Because of the babe?"

Dinah riveted her angry gaze to Poppy. "It wasn't my fault. My employer made me, said I would lose my job if I didn't let him."

The rage radiating from Dinah sparked in Poppy and caught fire. "Who did this?" she asked, her tone low and furious.

Dinah clenched her jaw and viciously picked up her teacup, sloshing droplets onto the bench and floor. "Doesn't matter."

"It does." Poppy wanted to confront the man herself.

"And what would you do?" Dinah asked, arching a dark blonde brow.

Shoulders drooping, Poppy frowned. Sometimes being a woman made one feel utterly helpless. If she were a man, she could at least call the blackguard out. She turned to Dinah in sympathy. "I'm sorry."

"I went home, but my parents didn't want me either. A neighbor took me in until everyone started to shun her." Dinah sniffed, then coughed. It took her a moment to control the spasms, but not as long as when she'd first arrived. She sipped her tea and set the cup back down. "I don't want the babe. It's been nothing but a burden to me."

Poppy stared at her. She didn't want the child? "You can't mean that. A child is a gift."

Dinah blinked at her. "What has this wretch given me but heartache and poverty? I lost my job, my place. I have no prospects."

Hearing her refer to the babe in such a way twisted Poppy's heart, and yet she could see the woman's perspective. The man—and the resulting child—had robbed her of what little choices she'd had.

"Hartwell House is the place for you. Mrs. Armstrong helps women just like you."

Dinah's eyes flashed with challenge. "There's no room."

"We'll make room." Poppy was determined to help this woman. "When the babe is old enough, you can go back into service. Perhaps we can even hire you here at Darlington Abbey."

Dinah shook her head vigorously. "No. I won't work in domestic service ever again."

Poppy couldn't blame her, but it would be different if she was employed here. "You'd be safe at Darlington Abbey. And you could have your babe." Poppy wasn't sure how they'd work that out, but they would. She had a vision of taking care of the child herself. The resulting ache was strong—and dangerous. She pushed it away.

"I said *no*." Dinah stifled a cough and grabbed another biscuit and thrust it into her mouth.

Poppy flinched inwardly. She didn't want to upset Dinah and perhaps provoke a coughing fit.

"All right, then. You could learn a trade at Hartwell House. Perhaps sewing."

"I don't want to sew. Or cook. Or clean." She gritted her teeth. Poppy was keenly aware of how trapped this poor woman felt.

Poppy angled herself toward Dinah and leaned forward. "What do you want to do?"

The fire behind Dinah's eyes dwindled. She looked down at her belly. "You'll laugh."

"I won't. I promise."

"Since I was a little girl, I wanted to be an actress." Her voice had turned soft and shy. She lifted her gaze but quickly averted it to some spot beyond Poppy. "My father took me to see a traveling troupe once. The actors were so beautiful, and they told such a magical story." She looked as if she were back there, reliving that moment.

"What was it?" Poppy asked, enchanted by Dinah's reverie.

Dinah blinked and looked at Poppy. "I can't remember, but I think it was Shakespeare. It was about a fairy queen and a king and lovers." She exhaled into a smile, and Poppy smiled too.

"Sounds like maybe *A Midsummer Night's Dream*."

"It was lovely. I wanted to be a fairy. Then I realized there are no fairies, so I'd have to be an actress so I could pretend to be one." She rested her hand on her belly. "I can't see how I'll ever do that now. It was a silly dream."

"No, it wasn't. Dreams aren't silly, and you shouldn't give up." She thought of her own, which would never happen, her gaze straying to Dinah's belly. *You shouldn't give up.* This was different—she couldn't make herself become pregnant, no matter how hard she tried or prayed or wished. She could, however, realize her dream another way. Right in front of her was a woman who said she didn't want her baby...

"Is there a good orphanage in the district?" Dinah asked, breaking into Poppy's selfish thoughts.

Orphanage? Then Poppy could volunteer to raise the child... *No.*

"I don't know, but I don't think you should consider that. I know this seems overwhelming to you now, but when you have the baby and see his or her face, you'll change your mind. You'll fall instantly in love." At least that was how Poppy imagined it would be. Her lungs contracted, and she fought to take a breath.

"I can't imagine it," Dinah said.

"That doesn't mean it won't happen. Give yourself—and the child—the chance. Doesn't he or she deserve to know its mother?"

Dinah picked up her cup and sipped the tea.

Poppy took her silence as an opportunity to continue her persuasion. "You could stay at Hartwell House, maybe even for a few years, until the babe is a bit older. You could learn a trade—something to do while you are trying to be an actress." Poppy had no idea how she would even go about that, but she was determined to encourage this young woman who'd been robbed of so much. "You could spend time reading plays. Perhaps you could organize the children there to perform something."

Dinah's eyes widened with horror. "Organizing children to perform? Is that even possible?"

A giggle escaped from Poppy, and she clapped her hand over her mouth. Then the most remarkable thing happened—Dinah started to laugh too.

After a long moment, their laughter abated, and Dinah yawned.

"You should get some sleep," Poppy said, rising. She picked up the tray, and Dinah nabbed the last biscuit with a smile. "I'll be right back to help you settle into bed." Poppy took the tray to Judith in the other room.

When Poppy returned, Dinah was already in bed with the covers pulled up to her chin. "I suppose you don't need me," Poppy said.

Dinah looked at her shyly. "Thank you. No one has ever made me feel like I mattered or that I could hope for things." She shook her head. "Never mind."

Poppy offered her a kind smile. "I understand. You *do* matter, especially to the babe you carry. I hope you'll think about what I said."

Closing her eyes, Dinah didn't respond. Poppy stood there for a moment, wishing there was something she could do to ease this woman's plight, but some parts of a journey were solitary. Poppy was learning this as she tried to find her way back to where she needed to be. Where she wanted to be. Whole and happy.

Poppy turned and grabbed her cloak and bonnet, then tiptoed from the room. In the main room, she set her bonnet on her head and pulled her cloak over her shoulders.

"Is she asleep?" Judith asked, coming to help Poppy don her cloak.

"Thank you," Poppy said. "Yes." She fastened the cloak, then tied the ribbon of her bonnet beneath her chin.

"I heard what you said to her. You're a kind-hearted person, my lady."

Judith might not think that if she could see inside Poppy. She wanted to be incredibly selfish, and she'd had the chance... Why hadn't she taken it? More importantly, how badly would she regret not turning this to her benefit, to doing what she'd advised Dinah—to pursue her dream?

Maybe she wouldn't have to. Dinah seemed quite committed to not raising her child. Giving her another option would be so easy and maybe even welcome. But Poppy wouldn't take advantage. Dinah was the child's mother, and Poppy would do everything she could to keep them together.

∾

*T*he early afternoon sun disappeared behind a cloud, lowering the already near-freezing temperature. Gabriel hastened his pace toward Dinah's cottage.

Though Poppy had only been gone a few hours, Gabriel missed her. Not for the time since she'd left to fetch her sister for the house party but for the past several days. She'd been sleeping in another bedchamber and spending a great deal of time at the cottage with Dinah.

He looked forward to when Poppy came home, to when they could return to the way things were. If that was even possible.

A lingering discomfort pervaded Gabriel's mind when he thought of what had caused the rift between them. *He* had caused it, with his lack of understanding for what Poppy had suffered and continued to endure. His relief was her pain. The unfairness of it nearly tore him in two.

Still, he found small comfort in knowing he wouldn't lose her the way he'd lost his mother and sister. The way she'd lost her mother.

Turning from the road, Gabriel made his way to the door of the cottage. Before he reached the threshold, Judith welcomed him inside.

"I saw you approaching from the window," she said.

He stepped inside, and she closed the door behind him. The interior of the cottage was warm and cozy, and it smelled of baking bread.

Gabriel inhaled deeply. "How long until the bread is done?"

Judith smiled. "Not long. I'll cut you a slice."

"If you insist." He grinned, then glanced toward the back room. "How is Dinah?"

"She's reading."

Gabriel blinked at her. "Is she?"

"Shakespeare. Lady Darlington brought *A Midsummer Night's Dream* the other day. She's had quite an effect on Dinah. She's actually considering keeping the babe now."

She was doing *what*? Gabriel masked his shock and disappointment. "What changed her mind?"

"Lady Darlington did."

She had? Gabriel was utterly confused. "I'm surprised. Dinah has been clear from the moment we met her that she doesn't want the child."

Judith nodded. "Lady Darlington has convinced her that she'd regret the decision, that as soon as the babe is born, Dinah will fall irrevocably in love."

That sounded like his wife. While Gabriel wanted the child for Poppy, he was moved by her selfless behavior. Taking the child would benefit them, but what of Dinah? What if she did regret not keeping him or her?

He'd come here intending to talk to Dinah about him and Poppy raising the baby. Now he couldn't do that, especially since Poppy had worked to persuade Dinah to keep it.

"I thought I heard voices."

Gabriel turned and saw Dinah standing in the

doorway to the bedroom. She wore a loose gown, but nothing could disguise the advanced state of her pregnancy. Dr. Fisk had told Judith the babe could come at any time.

"Good afternoon, Dinah," he said.

"Did you bring lemon biscuits?" she asked.

"I didn't." He glanced toward Judith. "Should I have?"

"Yes," Dinah answered. "Lady Darlington always brings them now."

"I didn't realize. I'll make sure you have some before nightfall." He walked toward her. "Judith said her ladyship also brought you something to read."

"She did. I like her. She's very kind."

"She is indeed. I am the luckiest of men."

"I'm going back to bed." Dinah turned and waddled back into the bedroom.

Gabriel followed her, not yet certain what he meant to say.

She climbed into the bed and looked slightly surprised, her brows arching, as she pulled the coverlet over her belly. "I thought you were going to get biscuits."

He smiled. "I will. Judith tells me you've changed your mind about keeping the babe."

Deep creases furrowed Dinah's brow. "I'm considering it. I asked Lady Darlington to stop bothering me about it, so if you're here to continue her assault, I'd ask that you don't."

"I won't." Conflict warred within Gabriel—he wanted to support Poppy, but he also wanted this baby for them. For Poppy.

For himself. Maybe he wanted to be a father more than he'd realized. His gut tightened, and he did his best to ignore the sensation.

"Dinah, I want you to know that whatever you

decide, your baby will be cared for. We'll make sure."

"You and Lady Darlington are the kindest people I've ever met, and that includes my own family." She shook her head. "I don't understand why."

And now Gabriel felt like a charlatan. His own desires and motivation aside, he did want to help her, even if she did keep the babe. "We don't turn our backs on those in need."

"You spend a great deal of time at Hartwell House from what I gather."

"We do."

"How long have you and Lady Darlington been married?" she asked.

"Three years in February."

"And you don't have any children of your own?"

He shook his head. "We do not."

"I wasn't sure. I assumed if you did, they were with a nurse or a governess. That's what you folk do."

Gabriel knew she was speaking from experience—with "you folk." "Were you a nurse? Or a governess?"

"No, I worked in a scullery. And as a maid."

"Did you?"

Dinah narrowed her eyes. "Lady Darlington didn't tell you?"

Gabriel kept himself from wincing. Poppy hadn't shared much with him of late. He decided there was no good answer to Dinah's question so he ignored it. "I'll make sure you have lemon biscuits."

"Hand me my book before you go, please."

The tome, from his library, sat on the bedside table. Well within reach, but she'd have to push up to get it. Gabriel handed her the play. "*A Midsummer Night's Dream* is my favorite Shakespeare."

She set the book on her belly, for she had no lap. "I saw it performed once when I was a child—by a traveling troupe of actors. Reading the words, I can see the play again in my mind."

For the first time, he saw joy in the depths of her usually apprehensive gaze. She looked like that talking about a play, but he'd never seen that when she spoke of her baby. He wondered if Poppy knew how Dinah had come to be pregnant. Hopefully, he'd be able to ask her. When she returned, and they went back to normal.

"Then I will leave you to it," he said, nodding toward the book.

He turned, and as he hit the threshold, she called, "Don't forget the biscuits! Please."

He looked back over his shoulder, but she was already reading. He watched her for a moment, thinking—shamefully—for the first time of her as a person with hopes and dreams and a baby she maybe didn't want. Or maybe she did. Either way, she was alone, impoverished, and without prospects. Yes, he must speak to Poppy about her. Whatever happened with the baby, they couldn't turn Dinah out without offering support. That wasn't who they were.

Assuming she survives.

The dark voice surfaced from the back of his mind. The petrifying fear that came when he thought of losing his mother and sister bubbled up. He was able to keep it at bay for the most part, but he'd come to know Dinah, and if she died… *When* she died. For he had every expectation that she would. And damn if that—his expectation—wasn't horrible.

Trying to banish the darkness, he strode into

the main room. Judith handed him a plate with a thick slice of bread slathered in butter. He didn't think he could force it past the lump in his throat. Still, he took the plate.

"I heard her ask about biscuits," Judith said.

"Yes, I'll have a groom bring some down later." First, he had to see if Cook even had any on hand.

Gabriel's insides roiled with unease. "How do you manage loss at Hartwell House? When people die, I mean."

Judith's eyes widened briefly. Lines creased around her mouth as she seemed to ponder his odd question. He was on the verge of telling her to forget he'd asked when she said, "It's difficult, particularly when we've come to know them well. However, we always see it as a blessing for them for they are no longer suffering. And, we hope, they passed in a place of comfort and love."

Tears stung the back of Gabriel's throat. He swallowed, praying he wouldn't humiliate himself in front of Judith. He took a bite of bread, not because he wanted to, but because it gave his body something to do besides surrender to grief.

The bread was delicious, and Gabriel was surprised when he eagerly finished the entire slice. The flavor, the simplicity, the care with which Judith had prepared it for him gave him comfort.

The room around him came into sharper focus as he saw with a clarity he'd never managed before. He handed the empty plate back to Judith. "Thank you. For everything." He smiled at her then turned and left.

He'd spent so many years fearing death that he'd failed to realize what he was truly afraid of, what he'd worked so hard to avoid—grief. The thought of losing Poppy had precluded him from living the way he ought, without preoccupation about things that he could not control.

He finally understood Poppy's perspective. Or, at least, he hoped he did. He loved her beyond measure, and that she'd suffered in her grief without him beside her—*truly* beside her threatened to break his heart.

Thankfully, he could fix this. He could show Poppy that the loss, the *grief*, was theirs together. She wasn't alone.

And neither was he.

CHAPTER 5

"*A*re you upset we left early?" Bianca asked as the coach carried her and Poppy away from Thornhill the day after the party began.

"Of course not. I only came to chaperone you," Poppy said. That wasn't exactly true. She'd also welcomed the chance to spend some time away from Gabriel. By leaving early, she was shortening her respite, but if she were honest with herself, she'd admit that she missed him.

Bianca smoothed her hand over her skirt. "And I appreciate it. Since you are already being so helpful, perhaps you can provide assistance with Calder. We are now in dire need of him to host the St. Stephen's Day party after today's debacle with Thornaby and the others."

"It was a debacle?" Poppy hadn't heard what precisely had gone on at the shooting competition that had been held at Thornaby's house party—she'd been too far away—but Bianca had said the host and his friends had bullied the Earl of Buckleigh. Whatever had happened had been enough to drive the Earl of Buckleigh away, as well as Bianca and Poppy.

"It was for Ash—and for me."

"You're calling him Ash again," Poppy murmured. They'd known the earl since they were children. He'd lived in Hartwell until he'd gone off to Oxford, after which he'd moved to London. He'd just come back this year upon inheriting the earldom from his cousin, something he'd never expected to do.

Bianca slid her an exasperated look. "You're pointing it out again."

Poppy smiled to herself. How she loved her sister. And how nice it was to be with her away from her own worries.

"It was especially awful because of St. Stephen's Day," Bianca said. "I'd hoped Thornaby could host the party at Thornhill—it's the closest estate to Hartwell after Hartwood."

"He won't host it?" Poppy asked, having missed that fact from earlier.

"I didn't ask him to. I *can't*." Bianca made a face. "He's horrid."

Poppy turned her head and stared at her sister. She'd jumped rather quickly and passionately to Ash's—*Buckleigh's*—defense. Was there something between them?

"Bianca, do you have a tendre for the earl?" she asked softly, her lips curving into a slight smile. How wonderful it would be if her sister fell in love. Poppy doubted Calder would be so fortunate. He was making himself rather unlovable with his stinginess and frigidity.

Bianca blinked, then turned her attention to the window. "Don't be absurd. We're old friends."

It seemed more than that based on Bianca's behavior, but Poppy wouldn't press the matter. She remembered falling in love with Gabriel. They'd danced at the holiday assembly, and she'd been immediately smitten by his charm and good looks.

He'd made her laugh, and she'd counted the days—two—until he'd called on her at Hartwood.

The three-year anniversary of their meeting was almost upon them, she realized with a bitter-sweet ache. Would they celebrate? Or would they still be at odds? She hoped not.

"Are you all right?" Bianca asked, fixing Poppy with an anxious stare. "I mean, I know things aren't—" She abruptly stopped and shook her head. "It's not for me to ask. I just want you to know that I'm here if you need me."

Poppy appreciated her sister's concern. It wasn't as if she was trying to keep anything from her, but why burden anyone else with her troubles? Especially when there was nothing to be done about them.

"Thank you." Poppy gently touched Bianca's arm. "You are the sweetest sister."

"Calder wouldn't agree," she said wryly, provoking a welcome laugh from Poppy.

"No, I suppose not. I do wonder if he will come around," Poppy mused. "To be more like how he used to be."

Bianca exhaled. "I can't see it happening, unfortunately, especially with him refusing to host the St. Stephen's Day party as all the other Dukes of Hartwell have done before him. I'm still going to try to persuade him, mind you."

"Of course you are. And if anyone can, it's you. But you're right. I do fear he's hardened into a forbidding shell, and that breaks my heart."

"He needs a wife," Bianca said, straightening her spine. "Someone who will manage him and make him feel again. What I should like to know is what made him this way." She looked over at Poppy. "Or do I just have a rosier idea of who he was before he went to school? I was rather young."

"No, you remember him correctly. He was kind and caring. He used to make jokes, if you can imagine."

"I can, actually. I remember giggling with him." Bianca frowned. "Which makes his behavior all the more maddening. And distressing." She turned her head toward Poppy. "What happened, do you suppose?"

Poppy thought she knew—or had a good idea, anyway. "I'm sure it was at least partly due to Felicity."

Bianca cocked her head to the side. "I'd forgotten about her. See, I *was* young. What happened?"

Felicity Templeton, now Garland, had lived in the village of Hartwell with her parents. When Poppy thought of how different her brother had once been, she always thought of him with Felicity. "Calder wanted to marry her. However, for reasons that have never been made clear to me, they didn't wed. She and her family moved to York."

"Her mother came back to Hartwell last year, after her husband died, I believe." Bianca glanced out the window. "I don't see her very often. In fact, I should look in on her. Perhaps I'll do that."

Poppy smiled. "You've such a caring heart. Let me know when you go, and I'll join you."

"Like when we used to visit Hartwell House together," Bianca said, grinning. "Do you remember when we first started going there?"

Poppy nodded. "Father said we read too many books and suggested we do something else."

Bianca giggled. "So we took our books to Hartwell House and read to the children."

"And then taught them to read," Poppy said with a hint of pride. They both still did those things, just not together. Of late, however, Poppy hadn't done them at all.

They fell silent for a few minutes before Bianca spoke up again. "Do you think Calder has had a broken heart ever since?"

"I suppose it's possible, but I'm not sure that's the case. Gabriel has told me all about Calder's behavior in London when he was younger. It doesn't sound as if he was pining for Felicity."

Bianca's brows arched. "I see."

Just like that, the mention of Gabriel drew Poppy back to her own problems. As much as she wanted to aid Bianca in her dealings with Calder, she needed to go home. All this talk of Calder and who he was before made her realize she was ready to be who *she* was before—who she wanted to be now.

Still, as they drove up the lane leading to Hartwood, she didn't want to abandon her sister's cause regarding the St. Stephen's Day party. "Bianca, do you want me to come in and talk to Calder with you?"

"I don't think it would matter," she said with resignation. "Anyway, he's often busy in his study —there's no telling if he'd even see us."

"Surely he'd come to dinner," Poppy said.

"To be honest, I'm not sure I have the patience for dinner with him tonight. Not after the events of the day."

The business with Ash had affected Bianca quite profoundly. Poppy kept that observation to herself.

After bidding her sister farewell, Poppy urged the driver to make haste so they would reach Darlington Abbey before it was fully dark.

～

*D*espite a succession of clouds, the light of the moon guided Gabriel back to the house. His belly was delightfully content from dinner at the cottage. Aside from making excellent bread, Judith also crafted a mouthwatering stew.

As he walked into the house, a giddy anticipation filled him. Tomorrow, Poppy would return. His excitement reminded him of the night before St. Nicholas Day when his family would exchange gifts. He'd barely been able to sleep, wondering what he'd receive on the morrow.

Deciding to have a glass of port before heading upstairs, he went toward his study and ran into the butler on the way.

"Good evening, my lord," Walker said. "Lady Darlington has returned."

The anticipation thrumming through Gabriel expanded. "Where is she?"

"Upstairs, I believe."

Gabriel was already striding toward the stairs before he remembered to thank Walker. As much as he'd enjoyed dinner at the cottage, Gabriel now wished he'd been at home instead. He took the stairs two at a time.

The fire in their sitting room burned low, and a single lantern flickered on the desk in front of the window. Gabriel went into their bedchamber and stopped short. Standing before the fire, her body silhouetted beneath her cream-colored night rail, was the woman he dreamed of. The woman who held his heart in her hands—precisely where he wanted it to be.

She turned, and he held his breath—both because of her beauty and because he didn't know what to expect. Would she turn him away? No, she was here, in their bedchamber, unlike the nights before she'd left.

"You're here," he whispered.

"I'm here. Bianca wanted to leave Thornhill early."

"Did something happen?"

"Thornaby and his friends—the ones you don't like—bullied our old friend Ash." She shook her head. "The Earl of Buckleigh."

Gabriel knew Buckleigh. They'd met on a few occasions in London, and Gabriel had encountered him in Hartwell since he'd become the earl. "I'd been meaning to invite him to dinner."

A half smile tilted her mouth, and Gabriel's heart flipped. "Have you? I suppose we've been busy. Or distracted." Gabriel's throat constricted, and she continued before he could gather himself to speak. "There was a shooting competition, and while I couldn't hear what was being said, Bianca could."

"Why is that?" Gabriel interrupted.

"Because she insisted on shooting and remained somewhat close to the competition after they deigned to allow her to have a turn—not *in* the competition, of course, but to demonstrate her skill."

Gabriel chuckled. "I'm not surprised she demanded equal opportunity. And good for her." His sister-in-law was perhaps the most fearless and self-possessed person he'd ever met.

"Whatever happened between the gentlemen upset Buckleigh enough that he left the party. Bianca insisted we do the same."

"To show solidarity?"

"I'm not sure. She says that she and Buckleigh are just friends, but she referred to him repeatedly as 'Ash.'"

"You just did the same," he noted.

"So I did," she said with a laugh. "We have known him forever, it seems. Beyond that, however, she was very upset by what happened. Passionately so, I would say." She gave Gabriel a direct stare. "The only man I feel passionately about is you."

Gabriel's pulse sped. His heart thudded, sending blood crashing through his ears. Had he heard her right? In a handful of steps, he stood before her. "Poppy, I think I understand what you've been going through. I didn't before. Or at least, I didn't want to. I should have shared in your grief —*our* grief—but I couldn't."

She took his hands in hers. "I know. I shouldn't have expected it of you. I know how deeply your mother's and sister's deaths affected you."

He didn't deserve her understanding. "Don't. I left you alone to deal with what was happening. Or not happening, as it were. I was too scared." He squeezed her hands. "I'm still scared."

She moved closer and brought her hands to his face, holding him as she looked up into his eyes. "I know, but you don't have to be."

He clasped her waist, holding her against him. "I wish I could change things. I wish I could fill you with a child. With ten children." She arched a brow at him, and he laughed softly. "Too many?"

"At once, yes," she said drily.

He grinned. "Not at once, then." Sobering, he wrapped his arms around her. "Scared as I am, I want to be a father, and I'm heartbroken I can't make you a mother."

Poppy stood on her toes, whispering, "My love. We are still a family." She kissed him, her lips soft and warm beneath his.

A dam of emotion broke inside him. He swept

her up against him and deepened the kiss, desperate to show her how much she meant to him and how sorry he was. But it was she who showed him—her hands twined in his hair as she pressed her body to his, offering herself in sweet surrender.

After a thorough, toe-curling kiss, she undressed him piece by piece, her lips pressing into his skin each time she revealed a new part of him. He cupped her head as she unfastened his fall to strip him of his last garment. "What did I do to deserve you?"

"Don't be silly," she said with a soft smile. "We deserve each other." She peeled his breeches away, exposing his cock. Then she dropped to her knees as she pulled the garment completely down his legs. Her hand encircled the base of his shaft as he worked to kick the breeches away.

Before he could tell her to stop, that he wanted to be the one to worship her, she took him into her mouth. Her dark curls fell across her cheeks as her head bobbed forward, her lips sliding over his flesh.

Gabriel thrust his fingers into her hair, holding her lest he spin away into darkness. He was aware only of her—the clasp of her hand, the gentle pressure of her thumb, the glide of her tongue, the heat of her mouth. His hips moved, and he had to work to keep from thrusting into her.

Suddenly, it was too much. He withdrew from her and bent to scoop her into his arms. He bore her the few steps it took to reach the bed, then he laid her down and climbed between her legs.

He reached for the hem of her night rail, but she was already tugging it up, revealing herself to him inch by inch. He smiled to himself as she went slowly on purpose. It had been a long time since she'd seduced him.

The moment she bared her sex to him, he bowed forward. She spread her legs to him, but he put his palms against her thighs and pushed them farther apart, opening her to his gaze completely. She was so beautiful with her bright pink lips and glistening folds. He was humbled by the offering of her body and just knew that the fault of their childlessness had to lie with him.

"Gabriel?" she asked softly.

He looked up her body where she had the night rail gathered at her waist. She'd brought her head up to look down at him, her gaze heavy with desire but also tinged with concern.

"Take it off," he rasped.

She pulled the garment the rest of the way up her body, lifting from the bed and then whisking it over her head. The cotton floated away, but he was fixed on her breasts, so full and round and tipped with soft, blush-pink nipples. They tempted him, but he was already committed, the scent of her arousal luring him back to her sex.

He buried himself in her, using his tongue and fingers to tease and fill her. Her whimpers were a song, urging him to give her more. He curled two fingers into her, finding that sensitive spot that sent her spiraling into ecstasy. Her legs quivered and her muscles clenched around him, signaling her release. She cried out, and he suckled her clitoris, drawing out her pleasure until she begged him to stop.

He looked up at her as she tugged on his hair. "You really want me to stop?"

"I want you inside me," she said.

"I was," he argued with a smile.

Her heavy-lidded eyes slitted with impatience and lust. "Not that part of you. Your cock."

She didn't often use coarse language, but God,

when she did, he nearly came undone. He prowled up over her body, lavishing kisses upon her flesh at intervals until he reached her breasts. There, he stopped and feasted on her until she writhed beneath him.

"You're taking too long," she said, breathless.

"The best things are worth waiting for." He drew her nipple into his mouth, sucking hard for a moment before licking along her pearlescent skin. "I like it when you talk to me. And say things like 'cock.'" He lifted his head and grinned at her.

One of her brows arched in that playful fashion he loved. Then she shoved at his shoulders, pushing him over and pinning him to the bed as she straddled his hips. "Put your *cock* in me now."

"Yes, my love." He grasped his shaft and positioned it at her sex. She lifted off him and covered his hand with hers, guiding him into her wet sheath. Bearing down, she covered him completely, drawing him deep into her sex. She closed her eyes, her body growing taut as he filled her.

Then she began to move. How he loved watching her like this—the slender column of her throat, the lines of deep pleasure etched into her face, the sway and bounce of her breasts as she pumped herself on him.

And then rapture claimed him. He gripped her hips and thrust up into her, losing himself in her sweet heat. She fell forward with a cry, grinding against him, bracing herself over him. He licked at her nipple, drawing her breast into his mouth, and she came apart around him.

Over and over, she bore down on him, her moans and whimpers driving him toward a climax that threatened to rip him in two. He held her tight as she collapsed over him, finishing with a rapid series of strokes and then cradling her close to his heart.

He kissed her temple, her cheek, her jawline. "I love you, Poppy."

She lifted her head and looked at him. "I love you too, but is that enough?"

CHAPTER 6

*T*he look of distress in Gabriel's eyes spurred Poppy to lean down to kiss him. She pulled back and caressed his cheek.

"That didn't come out quite right," she said. She drew in a breath and tried to formulate the words she needed to say to properly convey her emotion. "What you said earlier—" She couldn't bring herself to ask if he was truly heartbroken. "About having children—"

He slipped his hand into her hair and cupped her head. "Loving you, and you loving me, is all I need. If this is all we ever have, it is more than enough. More than anyone can hope for."

Emotion clogged her throat so she could only nod. She kissed him again, finding comfort in his embrace. It had seemed so long since she'd done that. He turned with her so they lay facing each other on the bed.

She nuzzled close against his chest. "I don't want to be melancholy about it anymore. I may always feel sad, but that can't be the ruling emotion in my life. Hearing you say that just the two of us is enough makes me so happy."

He tensed, and she wondered if she'd said

something wrong. She pulled back so she could see his face. "What is it?"

"Would you consider fostering a child?"

Dinah and her baby instantly came to Poppy's mind. "Yes. Did you have a child in mind?" She held her breath, wondering if he'd thought the same thing as she.

"I do. I did." His brow creased. He pushed up and pulled the bedclothes back so they could slide beneath them. Then he sat against the headboard. "I need to tell you the entire truth about Dinah."

She sat up and faced him. The covers settled around her waist, and a shiver twitched across her shoulders. "Can you reach my night rail?" she asked.

He slipped from the bed to fetch her garment, and she took the opportunity to marvel at his firm, rounded backside.

He helped her don the night rail before resituating himself in bed and continuing. "When I met Dinah at Hartwell House, it's true that Mrs. Armstrong didn't have space and that I wanted to help. What I neglected to tell you is that I'd hoped to persuade Dinah to allow us to raise her child. She'd already said she didn't want it, so I thought I would be offering her a welcome alternative." His gaze was heavy with regret. "That's why I didn't tell you about her coming to the cottage. I didn't want to get your hopes up in the event she declined. Or worse—if something happened to her and the baby."

"Oh, Gabriel." She took his hand in hers, wanting to draw his anxiety away. "I considered this too. But I felt selfish even thinking of it."

"Is it selfish if our need solves her dilemma?" he asked.

"I wouldn't want her decision to be based on our need."

"But she'd already decided she didn't want the child."

Poppy didn't think she could make that decision, not before giving birth. "I have to think she'd regret giving the babe away. How can she not look at his or her face and fall instantly in love?"

He traced his thumb over her hand. "That's what you would do."

"I would already be in love," she said softly. "From the moment I knew the babe was growing inside me, I would be lost." She watched as apprehension darkened his eyes and lined his forehead. Reaching up with her free hand, she brushed her fingertips over his brow. "I know that frightens you—the specter of what could happen. But I can't live in fear. *We* can't."

He nodded slowly. "I know that. Here." He tapped his temple. "But here…" He lowered his hand to his chest and pressed his palm against his heart. "Anyway, I don't think it matters as I believe she's changed her mind. You were quite persuasive."

She couldn't tell from his tone how he felt about that. "Are you angry?"

"How can I be when my wife is the most thoughtful person in the world? That you would ignore your own desire to save a woman from a lifetime of possible regret is the epitome of kindness and selflessness."

Poppy chewed her lower lip, suddenly worried about Dinah's future, and more importantly, that of her baby's. "I fear I will be the one to have regret," she admitted quietly. When he looked at her in confusion, she explained. "Dinah wants to be an actress. How can that be a good life for her or her child?"

Gabriel's dark gaze flickered with surprise. "I know nothing about the profession, but I imagine it's difficult."

"I tried to persuade her to stay at Hartwell House until the child is a bit older."

"You're hoping she'll change her mind about becoming an actress in that time?"

"Or at least wait." Poppy shook her head. "I don't know. I just didn't feel right trying to take the child, even with her saying she didn't want to raise it."

He tipped his head to the side, his thumb stilling on the back of Poppy's hand. "What if we offered her an option? If she knew that her child would be well cared for—*loved*—she may choose that over bearing the burden on her own."

His suggestion made perfect sense, but uncertainty lingered in her mind. "It still feels rather self-serving to me."

He gently squeezed her hand, conveying his understanding and concern. "Whatever happens with Dinah, I want to help her. We will see her and the babe settled. Are we in agreement on that?"

She loved him so much. "We are."

"And if Dinah does decide to raise her child, there are many other children who are in need of help. We will undoubtedly find one—or ten"—he flashed a smile—"to foster."

Poppy leaned toward him and pressed her lips to his for a soft, lingering kiss. "Thank you," she whispered as she pulled away. "I love you."

"Not nearly as much as I love you, and don't try to dispute that."

She laughed softly. He always told her that. "I

never do. Which isn't to say I agree." She gave him a saucy smile.

"Keep looking at me like that, and I'm going to roll you over and show you just how much more I love you."

Desire curled through her. "Promise?"

With a growl, he wrapped his arms around her and tumbled her back until she was flat against the mattress, his body covering hers.

"Wait," she said, suddenly breathless and quite happy to be. "I'd like to go to Hartwell House tomorrow. It's been too long."

His eyes, dark with passion, softened. "Of course. I would love to take you—if you want me to."

"There's no one I'd rather go with." She curled her arms around his neck and pressed her breasts up against his chest. "Now kiss me and whatever else you have planned."

"With pleasure." He grinned before claiming her mouth and stealing away thoughts of tomorrow.

~

*A*s it happened, the weather did not allow them to visit Hartwell House the next day. Or the day after. Trapped inside due to snow, they had no trouble making the best of their time. Though they did venture out for a walk in the snow—and a snowball fight that deteriorated into rolling around in the snow, which necessitated a shared bath. It was a delightful two days, truly the best Poppy could recall in recent memory.

Before going to Hartwell House, Poppy made a visit to the cottage to see how Judith and Dinah had fared in the snow. Plus, she'd wanted to speak with Dinah about her choices.

Poppy waited for Dinah to eat the first of the lemon biscuits she'd brought before launching into her proposal. "Gabriel tells me you've changed your mind about raising the baby. That's wonderful news."

Seated in the chair by the fire, Dinah looked as though her belly was taking over her body. Though it had only been a few days since Poppy had seen her, she seemed markedly rounder. "Did he?" Dinah plucked up a second biscuit. "I said I was thinking about it. I haven't decided for certain."

"I still think you should," Poppy said, choosing her next words carefully. "However, if you decide for any reason that you cannot be a mother to the child, Gabriel and I would be—"

Before she could finish, Dinah spoke. "You want my baby."

Poppy hated the way that sounded, but it was true. She wanted a baby, and Dinah was going to have one. "We want to help you. And if that means raising your child as our own, we would be honored."

"You made a rather persuasive argument as to why I should keep him." Dinah laid her hand atop her belly. "Or her. But now you want me to give it to you?"

"No." Poppy shook her head. "I still think you should keep him. Or her."

"But if I don't want to, you'll take him. Or her." She picked up a third biscuit and held it between her thumb and forefinger. "What sort of help will you give me?"

Poppy and Gabriel hadn't discussed anything specific. "What would you want?"

"I've been thinking about what you said, about how being an actress might make motherhood difficult, especially since I don't have any money to fall back on. I have to think of the babe as well as me."

She really *was* changing her mind. Poppy's stomach dropped through the floor. She hadn't realized until that moment that she'd actually been hoping Dinah wouldn't listen to her, that she'd want to leave the child. And, oh, didn't that make Poppy the worst sort of person?

"Yes, you do," Poppy said. "I'm glad to hear you're considering it. As I said before, I'm sure you could live at Hartwell House. We'll make room." Or she could live here. Poppy would talk to Gabriel about it.

"I'm still not sure I want to live there. I'd rather do something more than learn to sew. I actually know how to sew…" She thrust the biscuit into her mouth and stared into the fire as she chewed.

Poppy had spent enough time with Dinah to know the young woman was smart. Judith had just told Poppy that Dinah had read *A Midsummer Night's Dream* three times and was starting on her fourth. "Shall I bring you more Shakespeare to read?" Poppy offered.

Dinah swung her head back to look at Poppy, her eyes momentarily wide. "Yes. Please."

An idea came to Poppy. "Dinah, do you know how to do sums?"

"I do." Her brow furrowed. "Why?"

"I've long thought that Hartwell House should have its own school. Perhaps you could be the teacher."

Dinah's gaze moved from Poppy's and became slightly unfocused. After a moment, she blinked. "I'll think about it."

Every time Poppy glimpsed what was probably the real woman buried beneath the burdens of her young life, Dinah shuttered herself. It was as if she'd practiced hiding and didn't dare emerge.

Kindness. That was what she needed. And Poppy was determined to give it to her.

"Yes, you think about it," Poppy said sunnily as she stood, "There are more lemon biscuits if you want them."

Dinah sniggered. "Of course I will want them." She looked up at Poppy. "Thank you."

"You're welcome. I'll have a groom bring some Shakespeare." Poppy would make a few selections from the library before leaving for Hartwell House. She bid farewell to Dinah and then to Judith.

A while later, she and Gabriel were on their way to Hartwell House. "Thank you for delaying our departure," Poppy said, drawing the woolen blanket more securely about their laps as Gabriel drove the gig.

"What were you doing in the library?"

"Gathering more books for Dinah. She's on her fourth reading of *A Midsummer Night's Dream*, so I offered her something new."

"Thoughtful of you, but that is unsurprising." He tossed her a smile. "They were not troubled by the snow?"

Poppy shook her head. "Judith said Dinah even went outside."

"That's something." It was, for she mostly stayed in the cottage even though her cough was completely gone.

"I spoke to her about the babe. She is strongly considering keeping it now. I encouraged her to do so." She hesitated as she recalled her feelings of disappointment. She didn't want to bring that up to Gabriel, not when she was trying so hard to have a positive outlook. Focusing on that instead, she continued, "I came up with an idea for Dinah. She is not keen on living at Hartwell House and learning to clean or cook or sew. She's already worked as a maid, and that ended horribly."

He slid her an inquisitive glance. "She told me she was a maid, but I don't know what happened to her."

"After being elevated to upstairs maid, she drew the unwanted attention of her employer. He didn't give her the option of declining his advances."

Gabriel's jaw flexed, and his voice dropped to a low hum. "Who is he?"

"She didn't tell me." Poppy touched his sleeve. "Anyway, what would we do? It's not as if he would wed her, and I can't say I'd want him raising the child."

"I could call him out. Or beat him silly." He nodded. "Either would be satisfying."

"My beloved to the rescue." They exchanged a heated look.

"What was your idea?" he asked, turning her mind back to their conversation instead of how much she loved him.

"I was thinking about how much she likes to read, and how astounding it is that she loves Shakespeare. So I asked if she knew how to do sums. She does."

"What's going on in your shrewd mind?"

"We've discussed Hartwell House's need for a teacher. Perhaps she could take the position."

Gabriel looked over at her in open admiration. "Never say your sister has all the cleverest ideas. That's positively inspired."

Poppy sat taller in her seat. "Thank you. I hope Mrs. Armstrong is supportive."

"I'm sure she will be. As you said, we've been talking about this for a while now. This is a perfect solution—Hartwell House has a need and so does Dinah."

"She hasn't agreed to the position yet. She's thinking about it. I think she will." Poppy couldn't see how she could turn her back on such an opportunity.

"I'm sorry," he said softly, his gaze trained on the road ahead.

"Why?"

"Because it truly seems the baby will remain with her. Are you disappointed?"

"Yes," she admitted. "I don't want to be, but there's no help for it. Still, I think it's the right thing. And you're right, we'll find a child who needs us, and everything will turn out as it should."

Gabriel didn't respond, and they rode in silence the rest of the way to Hartwell House. When they arrived, Mrs. Armstrong was overjoyed to see Poppy.

"I'm so pleased to have you back again, my lady." Mrs. Armstrong beamed at her. "We've much to discuss. But first, I must speak to his lordship." She turned, grimacing, to Gabriel. "The snow caused a few new leaks. I just don't know how much longer this poor house is going to keep standing. You do your best to fix what you can, but a refurbishment is needed, and there's just no money." She waved her hand. "Never mind that for now. Can you please take a look at the corner in the dining hall? It bore the worst of the damage."

"I'll see to it." Gabriel took himself off.

Mrs. Armstrong turned to Poppy, her smile bright. "You are looking quite well. Are you?" Though her smile remained, lines fanned from her eyes and furrowed her brow.

"I am, thank you. I must apologize for staying away for so long. It was incredibly selfish of me."

Mrs. Armstrong looped her arm through Poppy's and led her from the entrance hall to her small sitting room to the left. Releasing Poppy's arm, the older woman took her hand instead as she faced her. "You are anything but selfish. I can well imagine what you've been enduring."

"You can?" Poppy had never talked to her about her troubles.

With a nod, Mrs. Armstrong motioned for Poppy to take one of the chairs near the hearth where a fire blazed. When Poppy was seated, Mrs. Armstrong sat in the other chair.

"Mr. Armstrong and I never had children."

Poppy knew that, or at least that she and her husband didn't have any living children. She realized she didn't know the particulars. "Have you never even been pregnant?"

Hands clasped firmly in her lap, Mrs. Armstrong shook her head. "And it wasn't for our lack of trying." She winked at Poppy. "Sometimes, however, we are meant to do other things. We were meant to open our home to women, including those with children, in need. Through that endeavor, we fostered a few children ourselves, including Judith."

"I didn't realize she was your foster child."

"She and her mother came to us when Judith was four. Her mother passed a few years later, and Judith remained. While we aren't an orphanage, in some instances, when the child had nowhere else to go, Mr. Armstrong and I kept them here. With Judith, I was just so attached to her, as she became attached to us when her mother was ill."

"I'm so glad you were there for her. Judith is a lovely young woman."

"She is," Mrs. Armstrong noted with pride. The pride of a mother. In that moment, Poppy glimpsed a future in which she didn't feel sad or... less. She wanted that future to start right now.

"I tell you this," Mrs. Armstrong continued, "because there are so many children who need a home and security. They need a family."

"I was just thinking that," Poppy said softly. "Thank you. Gabriel and I have discussed fostering a child." Or children. Why would they stop at just one?

"I'm glad to hear it." Mrs. Armstrong's blue gaze turned hesitant. "Dare I ask if that's why he took Dinah in?"

"Partly. He also just wanted to help—her and you. We know you are out of empty beds at present."

"We are, and the condition of the house is becoming a problem. I fear we need some big repairs." She looked as though she was going to say more but then snapped her mouth closed.

Poppy knew what was on her tongue. The same thing was in her mind. "Things have become more difficult since my brother withdrew the support of the dukedom after he inherited." She clenched her jaw as she thought of how he'd ceased giving the money their father had given to Mrs. Armstrong for Hartwell House. He'd said he needed to review the ledgers to determine if such charity could truly be afforded. As far as she knew, he hadn't made a final decision. "I will press him on the matter. In the meantime, we will pledge more support." Gabriel wasn't as wealthy as Calder, but he was committed to helping those less fortunate.

Mrs. Armstrong shook her head. "You both already give so much—money and time. Now, back to Dinah. Is she going to let you raise the baby?"

The blunt question took Poppy slightly off guard, but why shouldn't Mrs. Armstrong speak plainly? "I don't think so. I've been working to convince her to keep the child."

"You have?" Mrs. Armstrong asked with surprise.

"As someone who seeks and values motherhood, I worried she would regret not keeping the child."

"She didn't strike me as particularly motherly, but then Judith's missives have painted a picture of a young woman who fell victim to unfortunate circumstance."

"Judith has been writing to you about Dinah?"

"Yes. It sounds as though Dinah has perfected quite a bravado." Mrs. Armstrong cocked her head to the side. "Do you share that sentiment?"

"I can certainly see it. She hides her true self quite deep, I think. She's read *A Midsummer Night's Dream* several times."

Mrs. Armstrong laughed softly. "Judith mentioned that."

"She's good at sums too," Poppy said. "I wonder if she might fulfill the role of schoolteacher here at Hartwell House."

Mrs. Armstrong stroked her cheek in thought. "Oh, to finally have a school… Do you think she could?"

Poppy lifted a shoulder. "It's worth trying."

"It certainly is." But Mrs. Armstrong's expression dimmed. "I just don't know where we would house the school or her—and her child. We are fair to bursting at the seams."

"Let me discuss it with Gabriel." And Bianca— she would likely think of something. While Gabriel had noted she didn't have *all* the ideas, she did conjure a great many of them.

"Mrs. Armstrong!" A boy ran into the sitting room, his face pale. "There's a fire!"

Mrs. Armstrong leapt to her feet as the color drained from her face. Poppy rose, legs trembling and heart pounding.

"We need to get everyone out," Mrs. Armstrong said, sounding dazed.

"Not here," the boy, who was perhaps eight or nine, said. "It's over at Shield's End. Lord Darlington just left to go help. He told me to come tell you."

Shield's End was a house—and former farm—that belonged to Ash. It had been his family home before he'd become Earl of Buckleigh. "At least no one is living there right now," Poppy said with relief. Still, it was horrible.

Mrs. Armstrong laid her hand against her chest and closed her eyes briefly. "You gave me a fright, Michael. Round up the boys, and we'll go to see how we can help."

He nodded, then dashed out of the sitting room.

"I'll take them," Poppy offered. Since Gabriel had gone, she wanted to go too.

Lowering her arm to her side, Mrs. Armstrong gave her a grateful smile. "Thank you."

Despite the effort it took to herd the half dozen boys who joined her to walk over to Shield's End, they arrived fairly quickly. Smoke was visible from Hartwell House, which sat a half mile away, but now, as they walked up the lane to the house, she could see flames licking up from the structure. Her heart ached at the sight. Ash would be devastated.

Poppy cautioned the boys to stay close behind her and not go near the house. She led them to the back, where a line of villagers were passing buckets from the well to try to put the fire out. It seemed a losing battle.

Then she caught sight of her sister standing with Ash as they watched the house burn. Though she wanted to go to them immediately, Poppy took the boys to the water line and put them into service first.

After ensuring they were well organized, she hurried across the grass. "Bianca!"

Bianca pivoted. Her eyes lit, and she threw her arms around Poppy. In her haste, she knocked into Ash. The hug didn't last long as Bianca turned back to Ash and clutched his arm. "Sorry, are you all right?"

He gave her a wry look. "I'm fine. You can hug your sister. I should go see how things are progressing. I fear it's going to be completely ruined." He nodded toward Poppy. "Lady Darlington."

"Lord Buckleigh, I'm so sorry," Poppy murmured.

He ducked his chin, his eyes sad, then took himself off.

Bianca frowned after him. "I hope he doesn't overtax himself. He already rescued those who were inside."

Poppy gasped. "I didn't think anyone was living there."

"They aren't, but—" Bianca groaned. "It's a long story that I shall tell you later. Suffice it to say that Thornaby and his pack of rascals are responsible for this disaster in the name of a *prank*."

Poppy gasped again, this time, lifting her hand to her chest in much the same way Mrs. Armstrong had. "Despicable."

"Indeed," Bianca said darkly.

A dozen questions ran through Poppy's head. She chose what seemed the most pressing. "Whatever are you doing here?"

"Ash and I happened to be passing by." She opened her mouth to continue, but Poppy cut her off.

"You and Ash. Happened to be passing by. How?" She put her hand on her hip. "Why?"

"We're betrothed!" Bianca's bright blue eyes gleamed with excitement despite the disaster happening a short distance away.

"You're what?" Poppy was surprised and yet she wasn't. "That was fast."

"Faster than you and Gabriel, yes, but as I think you told me at the time, when you know it's right, why wait?"

She *had* said that. Or something like it. Joy coursed through her, and she hugged her sister again, this time for longer as happiness flowed between them. When they parted, Poppy caressed her younger sister's cheek. "I'm so thrilled for you. I want to hear everything. How you 'happened' to be passing by with Ash, how he proposed, all of it." She glanced toward the burning house and then at the water line where Gabriel stood with Ash surveying the fire. "But perhaps later."

"Yes," Bianca said somberly. "Definitely later."

Poppy looked around again. "Why isn't Calder here? Or any of his retainers? Surely they can see the smoke from Hartwell."

"Maybe. The clouds have thickened since we arrived. We didn't see the smoke until we were close to the village." Bianca snorted. "I am not excusing him, by the way."

"Me neither." Poppy gritted her teeth. "Later, after you tell me all your good news, we need to discuss him."

"We do." Bianca's tone held a note of foreboding —for Calder. Poppy might have felt sorry for their brother if he hadn't become a complete and utter blackguard. "I'm afraid he was quite horrible today, and I was actually on my way to stay with you until the wedding. If that's all right."

"Of course it is." Poppy didn't know what Calder had done now, but was certain he deserved a good shaking.

Bianca turned her attention from the house and looked to Poppy. "Let us go and speak to the men and try to soothe them."

"Bianca, I am truly sorry for Ash's loss."

"I am too, but I am just grateful he is fine. The loss of timber and furniture is nothing when compared to the loss of a loved one."

Hearing her sister speak of her love for Ash and seeing the emotion evidenced in Bianca's eyes made Poppy smile. "Well said, sister. Well said."

CHAPTER 7

"*I*t's good that it started raining," Gabriel said, thinking of the largely burned Shield's End as he joined Poppy in bed that night. "What a day."

She snuggled up beside him, laying her hand on his chest, as he sat against the headboard. "It felt like a week."

Gabriel stroked his wife's shoulder and back. "Bianca is all settled?"

"Yes, though I wonder if she will actually sleep. She's rather worked up."

"The fire or the wedding?"

"Both. I told her to focus on the latter. I don't think that will be a trial."

Gabriel smiled through his weariness. "They seem very happy."

"They do."

"It happened rather quickly, didn't it?"

Poppy chuckled, her body vibrating against his. "That's what I told her. She reminded me of something I told her after we became betrothed. Something to the effect of when it's right, it's right."

He gazed down at the top of her dark head. Her curls were tamed into a plait for sleeping, but he knew from experience that he could unwind it in a trice. Perhaps he would if he wasn't so bloody exhausted... "Is that how it was for us?"

She looked up at him, her lips curling into a heart-stopping smile. "Yes. Don't you agree?"

"Right doesn't adequately describe how I felt. To me, it was destiny." Perhaps he wasn't as exhausted as he thought.

She pressed a kiss to his chest, and though he wore a nightshirt, he felt the connection as if his flesh were bare to her. Sighing, she lowered her head to his chest. "Is Shield's End completely destroyed then? It looked as though the newer wing survived."

The addition made in the last century to the medieval-aged manor still stood, but Gabriel had to think it was greatly weakened. "I'm not sure it can remain without the support of the rest of the structure, particularly with the winter ahead of us."

"I hope he'll be able to rebuild soon. I'm glad Thornaby is paying for it."

Gabriel snorted. "That's the least he can do." Upon learning the fire had been caused by a goat, which Thornaby and his friends had brought into the house as a prank on Buckleigh, Gabriel had wanted to force the man to make restitution. That he apparently didn't have to be made to do the right thing was a small victory.

"Yes, after putting goats in the house. Bianca said they did that to Ash at Oxford and thought it would be amusing to repeat the prank."

"Makes me glad I went to Cambridge."

She glanced up at him. "No one stooped to such idiocy at Cambridge?"

Gabriel let out a sharp laugh. "Not that specifically. Perhaps I *should* have gone to Oxford. I would have stood up for Buckleigh if I'd been there."

"Of course you would have. You're the most thoughtful man I know." She tipped her head back to look him in the eye once more. "Thank you for agreeing to stand up with Ash at the wedding."

"It's my honor. I'm just sorry your brother is being such a miserable pig." He flinched. "Forgive my description."

She patted his chest once. "In this case, I'll allow it. I may even call him that myself since he refuses to approve of Bianca's marriage." Bianca and Ash had gone to tell Calder of their betrothal, but he'd refused to grant permission for her to wed him. Legally, Bianca didn't need it, but she did if she wanted the settlement their father had left for her. "He's still denying support to Hartwell House. When did he become such a cold, unfeeling blackguard?"

Gabriel didn't have an answer. As long as he'd known Calder Stafford, he'd always been heartless. "Please don't think poorly of me, but I'm beyond caring about him when so many are affected by his cruelty."

"I can't disagree with you, but I do plan to talk with him about Hartwell House. It's unconscionable that the building is in need of repairs, there isn't enough room for everyone who needs shelter, and it's past time we founded the school."

Hearing her speak so passionately warmed Gabriel's heart. It seemed she truly was breaking free of her melancholy, and for that he was exceptionally grateful. He leaned down and pressed a kiss to the top of her head. "You can talk to him, but I daresay it won't matter."

"I have to try. The fact that he refuses to host St. Stephen's Day is bad enough." She sniffed. "Bianca and I will do our best to ensure the celebration at

Thornhill meets everyone's expectations, despite it being so far away."

It was only five miles, but for many of the villagers, it might as well have been London. Thornaby had apparently offered to transport people, and Gabriel planned to do the same. If Darlington Abbey weren't even farther from the village, he would have insisted on holding the party here.

"I'm glad that's sorted, at least," Gabriel said. "As for Hartwell House, I will do my best to complete the necessary repairs. Some help would not come amiss." He could use both hands and financial support. He already donated a noteworthy sum to Mrs. Armstrong annually.

"I was thinking we should raise funds at the Yuletide Assembly. Bianca and I can surely persuade people to donate. We should squeeze Thornaby until nothing comes out."

Gabriel laughed. "You're vicious when you're on a mission. And that's a splendid idea—raising funds at the assembly, I mean."

She rotated her body so that her breasts were pressed against his chest and side and looked up at him with a saucy smile. "You don't agree with us bleeding Thornaby dry?"

"I'd actually pay money to see that."

Her eyes sparked. "Another way to raise funds!"

He laughed again. "Yes, though none of this solves the issue of providing additional room for Dinah and anyone else who comes along, nor does it address the school."

Her mouth tipped into a half frown. "I know. Watching Shield's End burn, I was thinking it could have made a marvelous extension of Hartwell House."

"Indeed it would have." He lightly massaged her neck.

"You're assuming Dinah wants to stay," she said softly, laying her head back on his chest.

He assumed nothing. He *hoped* she wouldn't, actually, that she would give her baby to them to raise. But he didn't voice that. "You've done your best to convince her."

Poppy ran her fingertip along the neck of his nightshirt. "You sound a bit disappointed."

Damn. "I'm not." *Yet.* "We should invite her to reside in the cottage for as long as she needs, though I'm sure Mrs. Armstrong would like to have Judith back at some point."

Sliding up his body a few inches, Poppy pressed a kiss against his collarbone. Exhausted or not, his cock didn't care as it stirred to attention. "You're the sweetest man. I'll let her know tomorrow. I plan to visit in the morning because I don't know how much time I can spend there over the next few days. There's much to do to prepare for Bianca's wedding."

Gabriel worked to ignore the desire swirling through him. They were both tired. "Mmm."

"I wanted to tell you what Mrs. Armstrong said to me today," she said softly, stirring him from his preoccupied haze.

"What's that?"

She pushed up to a sitting position beside him, her body angled to his. "She encouraged us to foster a child—or children. That's what she and Mr. Armstrong did. I didn't realize Judith has been with her since she was four."

"I didn't realize it was that long either," Gabriel said.

"She believes we'll have a family when it's

meant to be." Poppy's entire face beamed with warmth—and love. "I believe that too."

He clasped her waist and pulled her atop him so she straddled his hips. "I believe I married the most spectacular woman who will undoubtedly make all my dreams come true."

Her eyes narrowed provocatively as she pressed her pelvis down against his. "And what is your dream right now?"

He held her tight and moved her over his rigid erection. "I think you can probably tell."

She curled her arms around his neck and gave him a smoldering smile. "Good, because that's mine too."

~

*B*ianca's wedding the day before had been lovely and wonderful, even without the presence of their brother. Or maybe because of it. Poppy thrust him from her mind. Thinking of him only made her angry, and she was determined to be positive and pleasant. It was, after all, Christmastime.

Today was St. Nicholas Day, and already Darlington Abbey was adorned in greenery. Poppy made sure mistletoe was hung in key places, including Gabriel's study and the doorway between their sitting room and bedchamber. Plus at least a half dozen other places Gabriel would least expect. She'd done the same last year, and it had led to a rather memorable afternoon in the orangery.

Poppy stood back and surveyed the greenery she'd just festooned around the drawing room at Hartwell House in preparation for the St. Nicholas Day party that would commence shortly.

"What's that smile for?" Bianca asked as she breezed into the room.

"Oh, nothing, just remembering something in years past." Poppy noted that her sister was positively glowing today, and why shouldn't she be? Seeing her thus made Poppy so happy.

To think that just a fortnight ago, Poppy had been dreading the season because finding joy had just seemed impossible. Facing her disappointment and working through her grief—with Gabriel at her side—had made all the difference.

Bianca climbed onto a chair, and Poppy handed her one end of the pine garland the children had made that morning. "Last night, I was thinking about the space issues here at Hartwell House."

"On your wedding night?" Poppy shook her head while expelling a light laugh. "Of course you did."

"Can't turn my brain off, I'm afraid," Bianca said cheerfully. "Thankfully, Ash loves that about me. Now, I hope you don't find my proposal too forward, but I would think not since you are already giving shelter to someone for whom there wasn't room here."

Dinah. Poppy and Gabriel had visited the cottage briefly yesterday on their way home from the wedding festivities. Dinah had barely spoken to them, for she'd been extremely uncomfortable and had ultimately asked them to please leave her in peace. Judith had whispered that she suspected Dinah's time was coming soon.

A tremor of anxiety coursed through Poppy when she thought of the baby coming. Decisions would have to be made. There would be no more postponing the future—not for any of them.

A bead of hope worked its way through Poppy's

nervousness, but she refused to embrace it. She didn't dare.

She couldn't.

Poppy focused on her sister. "What's your idea?"

"Ash and I plan to open up a portion of Buck Manor to anyone who needs it. We have several rooms that aren't used, and they could provide a temporary home for a few souls until Shield's End is rebuilt."

"What a wonderful plan," Poppy said. "I wish we could do the same, but Darlington Abbey is not as large as Buck Manor. We should ask Calder to take people in."

Bianca nodded. "There are entire wings at Hartwood that he doesn't even step inside."

"He'll refuse," Poppy said flatly. "Though I suppose we should still ask."

"I don't think I've ever seen you so angry with him," Bianca said.

"I don't know that I ever have been. His behavior is deplorable."

"Can I presume you're speaking of your intolerable brother?" Gabriel strode into the drawing room, his arms full of packages, with Ash trailing behind, his arms also full of gifts for the children.

"What gave it away?" Bianca asked drily. "Poppy wants to ask him to help with housing people from Hartwell House as we plan to do at Buck Manor."

"A pointless endeavor," Gabriel said as Poppy moved to help him unload the gifts onto a table. "We should make him, however."

Ash deposited his armful of packages next to Gabriel's. "Is that possible?"

"No," Poppy and Bianca said in unison.

"Oh, let me try." Gabriel's whisper was soft and dangerous, his eyes gleaming with challenge.

Bianca set her hands on her hips and frowned. "He should be here. Our father would have been."

"He is not our father." And that made Poppy sad. Their father hadn't been perfect, but he'd been an excellent duke, a dedicated and admired leader in the community and in London. Calder, on the other hand, was feared. She supposed he *was* dedicated, but to only one thing: himself.

Gabriel looked to Bianca and Ash, who stood close together, their arms touching. "You plan to house people?"

Bianca nodded. "If it becomes necessary."

"It may. Mrs. Armstrong typically sees an influx of women in the winter, and, frankly, I'm concerned about the physical structure of Hartwell House. Three rooms are currently uninhabitable, and I can't see them being repaired until spring."

"Damn, if only Shield's End hadn't burned." Ash took Bianca's hand and addressed Poppy and Gabriel. "Bianca and I decided the house will be rebuilt specifically for the Institution for Impoverished Women."

Poppy gaped at him. "You can't be serious?"

"Never more," Ash said. "The house was sitting empty, and my mother will be staying with us. We were going to host the St. Stephen's Party there—before it burned—and I was glad to see it used for something that would benefit others. We'll consult with Mrs. Armstrong regarding what she'd like the new building to contain."

"That's just…" Gabriel shook his head. "It's incredibly generous."

"I know Mrs. Armstrong would like to have a school for the children who live there," Bianca said. "Ash would take that into account when he meets with the architects."

Poppy had an idea. "Or, and this may not work,

we could use Hartwell House as the school since Shield's End would be the new institution. If we can repair Hartwell House adequately."

Bianca beamed at her. "That's a marvelous suggestion."

Gabriel grinned as he regarded her with keen admiration. "You're just full of amazing ideas. And yes, we should be able to repair Hartwell House, especially if we're able to raise funds at the assembly next week."

"Oh yes, that is our intent." Bianca's gaze turned shrewd. "I'm thinking Thornaby and his friends should give until it hurts."

"As should Calder," Poppy said sourly. "Bianca, we're going to have to pay him a visit."

"Yes, we are."

"We'll come with you for fortification," Ash offered.

"I'm not sure if that would help. In fact, it may hinder us."

Mrs. Armstrong bustled into the drawing room, her dark gray skirts swirling about her legs. "Can you help bring in the refreshments? The children are beside themselves with anticipation. I think we need to begin the party." She smiled broadly. "Oh, to be young again!"

They went to help immediately, and soon the room was filled with laughter and gleeful conversation. Women and mothers and children alike opened gifts that Poppy and Gabriel and Ash and Bianca had provided. Watching their joy filled Poppy with contentment. She looked forward to the future and all they had planned.

Later, when everyone began to play games, Mrs. Armstrong drew Poppy aside. "Where is Dinah? I thought she was coming to the party."

"She wasn't feeling well. Judith thinks it may be almost time for the babe."

Mrs. Armstrong inclined her head. "I own I'm sad Judith isn't here. This is the first St. Nicholas Day we haven't spent together. I have a gift for her —perhaps you could deliver it?"

Poppy's heart pinched. "Of course. I should have sent someone to watch over Dinah so that Judith could come." She felt terrible she hadn't thought of that.

"Don't fret yourself. Judith would have said something if she thought it wise for her to come. I wager she thought she was needed with Dinah."

At that moment, one of the grooms from Darlington Abbey appeared in the doorway. He held his hat in his hand, and his face was reddened as if he'd been riding in the wind.

Gabriel went to speak with him, and Poppy watched as his features tensed. He nodded then turned, his gaze searching for Poppy, but she was already walking toward him.

"What is it?' she asked, her entire body swirling with apprehension. With expectation.

He clasped Poppy's hand, his fingers tight around hers. "Dinah has gone into labor. The babe is coming."

CHAPTER 8

*B*y the time they reached the cottage at Darlington Abbey, Gabriel's anxiety and apprehension were so high that he wanted to climb right out of his skin. He prayed Dinah and the baby would be fine. And then he prayed she would decide to let them raise her. Or him.

He shared neither of those hopes with Poppy.

It was nearly dark when they arrived. Another vehicle was parked along the lane. Gabriel recognized it as belonging to Dr. Fisk. Knowing the physician was here should have made him feel better.

It did not.

Gabriel helped Poppy from the gig. They hurried inside to escape the cold, but mostly to discover what was happening.

A wave of dread crested over Gabriel as they reached the front door. He hesitated.

Poppy must have sensed his fear. She turned to him and put her gloved hands on his cheeks, as she looked earnestly into his eyes. "Whatever happens, my love, we will be fine. *You* will be fine."

"I'm not worried about me," he said quietly, his voice a thin thread.

"I know." She gave him an encouraging smile and pressed her palms gently against his face. "And that is why I love you so. One of the many reasons." She stood on her toes and kissed him just as a scream rent the air.

Gabriel gasped against her mouth, his eyes flying wide as panic sliced through him. He remembered his mother screaming when she gave birth to his youngest sibling, a stillborn boy his father hadn't wanted to name.

Poppy opened the door and preceded him into the cottage. It was warm—warmer than usual—with a large fire blazing in the hearth. The flames were so high that Gabriel couldn't see through to the back bedroom.

"Good evening, Dorothy," Poppy said.

Who was Dorothy? Gabriel blinked and realized one of the maids from Darlington Abbey was tending the fire.

She turned and bobbed a curtsey to Poppy and Gabriel. "Good evening, my lord, my lady. Dr. Fisk stopped and picked me up on the way here. He said he needed an extra pair of hands because Mrs. Fisk wasn't able to come."

"Where's Judith?" Poppy asked.

"In the back with Dr. Fisk. I don't think it will be long now."

"We heard a scream." The words came from Gabriel's mouth, but he sounded as if he were standing outside his body listening to someone else speak.

"She's done that a few times now," Dorothy said, wincing. "I heard Dr. Fisk tell her that was all right."

Poppy moved to stand in front of Gabriel. She'd removed her hat and cloak, as well as her gloves. "Try to relax, my love," she whispered, removing his hat. "Why don't you sit?" She unfastened his great coat and moved around him to help him doff the garment.

He watched as she hung the items next to hers on a hook near the door. He felt as if he couldn't move. God, if this was how he behaved when a woman he barely knew gave birth, how would he be if Poppy were in this situation? He was immensely glad he'd never find out.

Before he realized what she was doing, Poppy had removed one of his gloves. After he removed the second, she took his arm and guided him to the settee near the fire. A few moments later, she returned with a glass of brandy, which she pressed into his hand.

Grateful, he lifted the drink. Another moan followed by a high-pitched wail filled the cottage. He jerked, and half the liquid in his glass splashed over his hand and onto the floor. "Bloody hell," he muttered. He needed to pull himself together.

Poppy rushed to wipe up the brandy from his hand and wrist, then did the same with the droplets on the floor. "Drink."

He didn't have to be persuaded. Downing the contents of the glass in one gulp, he welcomed the spiced fruit flavor. But it wasn't enough. He held the empty glass up for her to refill it. A moment later, she pressed it back into his hand. This time he sipped. And managed not to spill when a long, loud, shuddering moan seemed to shake the very walls of the cottage.

"Do you want me to go look in?" Poppy asked him softly.

He looked up at her and nodded. "Please."

She left him, and then he heard it—the beautiful, unmistakable sound of a baby's cries. The tension in him released, and he sagged back against the settee. He stared at the fire, unseeing, as he listened to the sounds from the other room—bustling feet, Dr. Fisk giving orders, that melodic cry.

Melodic?

He wiped a hand over his face and laughed at his pathetic state. After a few minutes, Poppy returned. "It's a girl," she said, grinning. "Dr. Fisk said the birth went well. Dinah is resting now."

"And the babe?" All the tension that had left Gabriel gathered once more, curling and tightening within him.

"Suckling." She quickly added, "There is no wet nurse." Had she read his mind? His first thought was that Dinah had made her decision, that she was going to keep her baby.

Her daughter.

Suddenly realizing he would never have a daughter who looked like her mother, Gabriel's insides turned to mush. His throat squeezed, and he forced himself to breathe.

Poppy sat down beside him. "Do you want to go, or would you rather stay for a while?"

"Stay." He had to know what Dinah meant to do. And he wanted to see the babe.

Gabriel sipped his brandy and Poppy sat quietly next to him, her thigh pressed against his. Dr. Fisk finally came from the bedroom, his ruddy face dappled with sweat.

"Good evening, my lord," he said with a bow. In his fifties, the doctor was a kind and generous man with a large family of his own, including a son who planned to become a physician. Dr. Fisk, often with his wife and a few of his children helping, cared for the women and children at Hartwell House without accepting payment.

Setting his glass down on a small table, Gabriel rose and shook the man's hand. "Good evening, Dr.

Fisk. Thank you for attending Dinah. I hear everything went as it should." He heard the note of question in his voice, despite Poppy already telling him things went well.

"Quite! Though rather, er, vocal, Miss Kitson was an excellent patient."

"She'll recover?"

"I have every expectation, my lord," Dr. Fisk said jovially as he glanced toward the glass of brandy. "I don't suppose I might trouble you for a nightcap?"

"I'll see to it," Poppy offered with a smile.

Gabriel suffered through a good half hour—at least—of chatting with Dr. Fisk before the physician returned to the bedroom once more. Then he took his leave with the promise to check in on the mother and babe in a few days.

The moment he left, Gabriel's anxiety climbed even further, and it took a great deal of effort not to ask him to come back. What happened if Dinah or the babe took a turn?

Dorothy came from the back room bearing a basket with soiled linens. "My lord and lady, if you'd care to visit briefly, you are welcome."

Poppy started toward the bedroom, then stopped, perhaps realizing that Gabriel hadn't moved. He stared toward the chamber in fright, unable to make his feet move.

Coming back to him, Poppy took his hand. "Are you all right?"

Somehow, he nodded. Then he took a step. And another. As they reached the threshold, he recognized a scent in the air, something he couldn't describe. Something he associated with despair. A memory came rushing over him.

His mother lying in the bed, her face pale, her body cold. He wasn't supposed to be there. But he'd wanted to see his beloved mama and tell her how sorry he was that his baby brother had died.

He took her hand. She usually squeezed his fingers and called him her "sweet boy." She did neither.

"Mama?" he whispered, standing on his toes so he could lean toward her form.

She didn't stir. He let go of her hand and found the stool to climb onto the bed. Just as he put his hands on the mattress to boost himself up, his father came in and yelled at him to get away.

"She's gone, boy!"

"Gabriel? Gabriel, can you hear me?" Poppy stood in front of him, her hands on his cheeks, her eyes wide, her words a desperate plea.

He blinked as he returned to the present, to this smell that wasn't quite the same but close. It could so quickly turn…

"She's going to die," he whispered, his gaze moving past Poppy to the bed where Dinah lay cradling her babe. Swaddled in blankets and nuzzled to her mother's chest, the girl was barely visible. Perhaps she was already gone…

Poppy pulled his head down, forcing him to refocus on her. "Look at me, Gabriel. You mustn't think like that. She's fine. And the baby is fine."

"Now. But you know as well as I do that can change."

"It can change for all of us," she said, keeping her voice low. But her tone was harsh. Honest. Fucking unavoidable. "You and I can leave tonight, be set upon by highwaymen, and killed. Or contract an ague and die in a fortnight. Or perhaps there would be a fire, and Ash won't be here to save us. Bad things happen, my love. They happen all the time. But so do good things. We must focus on those, pray for those, celebrate those. If we don't… What is there?"

He heard what she was saying and came to the same question—what is there? He watched as Dinah bent her head and kissed the babe, holding her to her chest. She smiled and whispered to the girl, every part of her radiating joy and love.

She was not going to abandon her daughter.

So much for good things. Steeling himself, Gabriel stepped around Poppy toward the bed. "You look well," he said, sounding surprisingly normal.

Dinah tipped her head up. She looked pale, but not dangerously so. Her eyes were tired, but her mouth seemed glued into a half smile. Indeed, he'd never seen her in such fine spirits.

"I have a baby girl," she said.

There was his answer. But he'd already deduced it. "So I heard. Have you chosen a name for her yet?"

Dinah looked down at her and shook her head. "I never allowed myself to think of a name. I didn't think I should."

Poppy had joined them at the bed, standing on the other side. "Why?"

Glancing toward Poppy, Dinah spoke in a soft, almost sad voice. She didn't sound quite like her-self—at least not the woman Gabriel had come to know. "I didn't think I would be a mother. I didn't think I should."

He had to strain to hear the last part. He looked over at Poppy, saw the flash of pain and disap-pointment in her eyes, and felt the emotions echoing in his heart. She covered them quickly, smiling at Dinah with warmth and understanding.

"Of course you should," Poppy said with honest encouragement. Gabriel knew that as badly as she wanted a babe, she would support this woman's choice to be a mother.

"I know you hoped—" Dinah snapped her mouth closed, her jaw tightening, and returned her attention to her daughter. She held the girl close, as if she were afraid to lose her. Gabriel would do the same if the babe were his.

Poppy touched Dinah's arm. "I hoped for you to find peace, to make a choice that you feel is best for you and the babe."

When Dinah looked back up, her eyes were full of tears. "You were right, my lady. I am in love. I can't ever let her go."

"Of course you can't."

Gabriel couldn't believe Poppy's voice didn't catch. He didn't think he could speak if his life depended upon it.

"I'm so glad we could help you become a mother and provide a safe haven," Poppy said, stroking Dinah's arm. "When you are recovered, we can talk of the future. Your future—yours and your daughter's."

Dinah nodded and dashed her hand over her eyes. "I've been thinking about what you mentioned before, about becoming a teacher at Hartwell House. I—I would like that very much."

Poppy's eyes lit with joy—true happiness amidst this crushing disappointment. "Wonderful! We will need to work out the specifics, but we have so many plans for Hartwell House, and now you will be a part of them."

"Thank you." Dinah looked from Poppy to Gabriel, her eyes welling once more. "I can't thank you enough—ever. You have changed my life. You have *given* me life. How fitting that this is St. Nicholas Day." She smiled down at her daughter. "If she were a boy, I would name her Nicholas."

"Why not Nicola?" Poppy suggested.

"Oh, that's perfect." Dinah tapped her finger lightly against her daughter's nose. The babe snuffled, and Dinah laughed softly. "Nicola, my love."

Gabriel needed to go. "Poppy, we should allow them to rest."

"Yes, we should." With a final pat to Dinah's arm, Poppy said goodbye and they left.

They spoke briefly with Judith, who planned to stay with Dinah for a few more days at least. Poppy said she would speak with Mrs. Armstrong about moving Dinah and Nicola to Hartwell House. Gabriel heard them discussing ideas about how to make that happen but wasn't listening to the words. He'd gone back to that room with his mother.

Somehow, he and Poppy were soon ensconced in the gig. He plucked up the reins and started toward the abbey, his muscles moving as if he were an automaton. After several minutes, Poppy exhaled as she pressed close to his side. "What a long day."

"I found my mother dead."

The words cascaded from his mouth like an avalanche of rocks that would crush him if he didn't flee. Gabriel had nowhere else to run.

Poppy stiffened beside him. He didn't look at her but could feel her gaze on him like the rays of the sun on a hot summer day. But he wasn't warm. The night was cold, and he was even colder on the inside. Absurdly, he wondered if this was how Poppy's brother felt.

"You never told me that," she said quietly.

"I only just remembered it tonight."

She put her hand on his thigh beneath the blanket she'd drawn over their laps. "That's why you went so deathly pale. I worried you were going to faint."

"It was the smell. Of birth, I suppose." He shook his head the faintest amount, his gaze trained on the dark road, barely illuminated by the lanterns hanging from the sides of the gig

"That triggered the memory?"

He swallowed as the recollection filtered back in small pieces—he didn't want all of it. "I only wanted to see her, to tell her how sorry I was that my brother had died."

"He was stillborn."

"Yes. My father told me I couldn't visit her, that she was tired and not feeling well. But I just had to see her. " His voice started to break. He gripped the reins, glad the journey was short and they were nearly to the stable.

"Gabriel." The anguish in his wife's voice nearly undid him.

"Please don't, Poppy," he barely whispered. "I can't."

He drove her to the side door and stopped the gig. "Go inside. It's cold."

"I'll go to the stable with you, and we can walk to the house together."

"No. Please go."

She turned toward him—he could feel her movements. "I'm not leaving you. Not like this. You're upset."

"Poppy, *go.*"

The sound of her breath drawing sharply into her mouth and the feeling of her body going ramrod straight beside him did nothing to ease the ache inside him. On the contrary, he only felt like more of a failure. She deserved a child, and he couldn't give her one.

She got out of the gig and walked inside, turning to look at him as she reached the door.

Gabriel couldn't meet her gaze. He should at least have helped her out of the vehicle, but he was too entwined in himself. In the painful past.

In the dismal future.

He drove to the stable and cared for the horse himself while the grooms managed the tack and vehicle. Moving slowly, he didn't care how long the task would take. He had nowhere he wanted or needed to be.

Yes, it was St. Nicholas Day. A day for giving and sharing. He'd never been more bereft.

❧

"*T*ell me how you're enjoying being married," Poppy said to Bianca as they drove to Hartwood. If she could manage to keep the conversation diverted away from herself, she would be able to keep from breaking down. And yet, she wondered if it might do her good to discuss her problems with someone. No, not with someone. With her sister.

Bianca laughed, and Poppy seized onto the glorious sound, basking in its joy and warmth. "It's only been a week. But it's quite lovely." She gave Poppy a knowing glance, and Poppy couldn't help but laugh too.

"I see," Poppy murmured. "I am glad you are content. You chose very well. Ash is perfect for you."

Grinning, Bianca situated her cloak around herself, almost preening. "Yes, he is. He's quite excited about the new Shield's End." She cocked her head to the side. "It will be strange not to refer to the Institution for Impoverished Women as

Hartwell House. Perhaps we should keep the name."

"Except Hartwell House will still exist as the school."

Bianca exhaled. "That's true. We shall simply have to adjust. Shield's End will be the institution and Hartwell House will be the school." She shook her head, smiling. "How lovely it will all be when it's completed." She looked over at Poppy. "I was so pleased to hear Dinah has agreed to teach the children."

The mention of Dinah sliced through Poppy, reopening the wound she'd been trying to heal over the past six days. Doing so was proving difficult, particularly because Gabriel barely spoke to her. He barely spoke to anyone. And he didn't sleep in their bed.

Poppy had visited Dinah and Nicola several times. They were doing quite well. Dinah was already managing her cottage, and Nicola was a large, healthy babe. Dr. Fisk was very pleased with their recovery. Judith would return to Hartwell House in a few days.

"She'll be wonderful in the role," Poppy said. "We've discussed how she means to proceed, and she's given the position a great deal of thought. She would like to begin after Epiphany, but I cautioned her to take things slow."

"Indeed. She has her hands full, I imagine." Bianca fell quiet a moment, but her gaze was fixed on Poppy. "Has it been difficult?" she asked softly. "Spending time with Dinah and her babe?"

Poppy tensed. "No." That was a lie. Why should she lie to her sister? "Yes. But I'm very happy for her—I'm glad she decided to stay and be Nicola's mother."

"That doesn't make it any easier." Bianca's brow

creased, and her mouth turned down as sympathy clouded her eyes. "I'm sorry."

"I'm most worried about Gabriel, actually." So much for avoiding the topic. "The birth brought up memories of his mother's death. He's been incredibly upset."

"Did it do the same for you?" Bianca asked.

Poppy shook her head. "I was not reminded of our mother. I don't remember her at all. Gabriel was much older than I was when he lost his mother." She stopped before she revealed how worried she was.

"You'll work through this," Bianca said with a confidence Poppy didn't feel. "I pray my marriage to Ash will be as loving and caring as yours is with Gabriel. You support and love each other." She gave Poppy a small, admiring smile. "It's lovely to behold."

Poppy blinked and then looked out the window. She knew Bianca was trying to help, but her words only reminded Poppy of how they weren't supporting each other right now. And how she wanted to be there for Gabriel. If he would let her.

Poppy sniffed and straightened her spine. "Let us discuss how we mean to proceed today. What do we hope to gain from our visit with Calder?"

They'd discussed paying a call on their brother and had decided it was past time. "We've so many things to talk to him about," Bianca said, pursing her lips. "Where to begin?"

"I should like to lambaste him for not attending your wedding."

Bianca curled her lip. "He did not approve."

"What palaver," Poppy said in disgust. "After I scold him about that, let us castigate him for refusing to support Hartwell House. It's in a shambles, and he could help fix it tomorrow."

"*Castigate?*" Bianca sniggered. "Why, Poppy, am I rubbing off on you?"

"It was bound to happen." Besides, Poppy had enough strife. She didn't need any more from her idiot brother.

"We should also mention the assembly. He really ought to attend."

"Why, so he can cast his dark cloud everywhere?" Poppy grunted softly. "My apologies. I am taking my frustration out on Calder."

"I can think of no one who deserves it more," Bianca murmured.

They arrived at Hartwood, and Truro, the butler, welcomed them warmly. "May I say marriage agrees with you, Lady Bianca?" He shook his head. "Forgive me, Lady *Buckleigh.*"

"It does, Truro," she answered gaily. "And please do not worry over propriety with *me.*" She waggled her brows at him, and he couldn't help but chuckle.

"And Lady Darlington, may I say how nice it is to see you."

"Thank you, Truro. I'm delighted to see you as well. I hope our brother isn't causing you too much distress."

Truro's gaze flickered with surprise and maybe…appreciation. "Not at all, my lady."

"You can be honest with us," Bianca said conspiratorially, leaning toward the butler. "We know how His Grace has been. And we're here to fix it."

"Well, you can try, my lady." His eyes widened briefly and he nodded once, keeping his head bowed for a slight moment.

Bianca inclined her head with determination. "We'll do just that. Will you let the duke know we're here? We'll await him in the drawing room."

Poppy and Bianca gave their outerwear to a footman, then showed themselves to the drawing room. Bianca looked about as if she'd never been there before. "It's strange to be here as a guest."

"Yes, it took some getting used to for me." Poppy wasn't sure if it was her current situation or Calder's frigidity, but she'd never felt more uncomfortable here.

"He hasn't even decorated," Bianca noted as she crossed to the hearth. "There should be boughs here. And mistletoe."

"My sisters have arrived."

The deep voice of their brother made them both turn toward the doorway. He filled it impressively with his towering height and wide shoulders. His frosty gray eyes surveyed them briefly, as if he wasn't entirely pleased to see them. No, "pleased" wasn't a word one would use to describe Calder, especially given the harsh lines around his mouth and the near-constant furrows cutting across his brow.

Bianca frowned. "You still need to work on your greetings."

"You need to work on a great many things," Poppy added, then inwardly winced. She hadn't meant to start like that—what was wrong with her?

She was angry. And sad. And in need of something she could *fix*.

Calder sauntered into the room and went to sit in a high-backed chair situated near a settee. He didn't invite them to sit. "Out with it, then. Since you came all this way. But do be brief. I am rather busy."

"With what?" Bianca demanded, marching toward him and dropping onto the settee. "You don't have a wife. You aren't helping Hartwell House. You aren't hosting St. Stephen's Day. What are you *doing*?"

"Being a duke." His ice-gray gaze was colder than a shard of ice, his tone supercilious.

Poppy moved to sit beside her sister. "Well, I am a married marchioness, and I still manage to dedicate time to Hartwell House. And St. Stephen's Day." And a host of other things.

"You're a woman."

Bianca narrowed her eyes at him. "Careful, Calder, or I'll chuck something at your head."

"If you both truly came to berate me, you've wasted your time." He started to rise.

"Do sit down," Poppy said. "Please. We want to speak with you about Hartwell House. It's in grave disrepair, and if you reinstated the support Papa gave, we could—"

"No."

Bianca reached over and clutched Poppy's hand, squeezing it. "Why not?"

"Because I haven't the funds."

"Nonsense," Bianca argued. "If Papa could afford it, why can't you? Have you mismanaged things so quickly?"

Calder's gaze grew—impossibly—colder. "How do you know he could afford it?" His voice was dangerously soft.

Poppy had the feeling she didn't know this man at all. Her anger began to give way to alarm. "Are you saying Papa mismanaged things?"

"I'm saying you don't know anything about the estate or what I can afford. Furthermore, you shouldn't be bothering me about it. You're both married now." He gave Bianca a terse look. "I should think you would pay all your attention to your husbands."

Poppy couldn't keep quiet. "Yes, we're married. Why didn't you come to Bianca's wedding? We know you were invited."

"I didn't approve of her choice of husband. He's a brutal pugilist who can't seem to control himself. Why would I support something which I cannot endorse?"

A low groan of frustration bubbled from Poppy's throat. "What has happened to you? Why are you so horrid, so unfeeling?"

He began to stand again, this time rising fully. "If there's nothing else…"

"There's plenty else," Bianca snapped. "Such as not hosting the St. Stephen's Day party. Did you know we were going to have it at Shield's End?"

"It burned down."

Bianca let go of Poppy's hand and stood, glaring at him. "Yes, and Ash thanks you for your concern." She took a step toward him. "Why won't you answer Poppy? What has made you like this? How can you turn your back on those in need? Several of the rooms at Hartwell House are leaking. The institution is bursting with residents. Until Shield's End is rebuilt, we have to make Hartwell House more habitable. You *must* help."

"I mustn't do anything. If you and your husband"—he tossed a glance at Poppy—"as well as you and yours want to waste your money on an endeavor that will provide no return, you are featherbrained indeed."

Poppy rose on shaking legs as she exchanged an incredulous look with Bianca. "Featherbrained?" they asked in unison, their voices climbing.

He shrugged. "There is nothing to be gained from coddling those less fortunate. The institution should be turned into a formal workhouse. In fact, I am looking into how to make that happen."

Their jaws dropped, and it was Bianca who found her voice first. "You can't. Mrs. Armstrong will never let you turn it into a workhouse."

"Well, I am the magistrate, and it's up to me to ensure our community is orderly. Hartwell House may not be allowed to continue as it is. The institution should be run by the parish."

"Hartwell House is not disorderly." Poppy sounded as if she were choking. And she supposed she was—on her brother's cruelty and disregard for those less fortunate.

Bianca touched Poppy's forearm. "Poppy, don't bother. I fear he's lost to us. Just look around you. There's no cheer. No warmth." She gave him a pitying look. "And to think I wanted to convince you to come to the assembly."

He twisted his lips into a frown. "What assembly?"

"The holiday assembly *in two days*," Bianca said. "We hold it every year. But then, you aren't usually here. You haven't been here in more than a decade. Now you're back, and you've completely destroyed our family's legacy."

Bianca went to him, standing just in front of him so he had to look her in the eye. "What happened to you?" she asked softly, trying to infuse her voice with care. It wasn't difficult. He was her brother. Somewhere in there was the boy who'd led them around the estate playing pirates.

He looked at her, but the connection was brief. His discomfort, his *antipathy* radiated from him like a stench that couldn't be scrubbed away. "Nothing."

"Felicity Garland is back," Poppy said, searching for the faintest reaction.

There. A slight flicker in his eyes. It faded so quickly she could have imagined it.

He blinked at her, tipping his head slightly as if annoyed. "Felicity who?"

Now she knew he was just lying. Poppy scoffed

and turned away from him. "Yes, I daresay he's a lost cause. Come, let us go. It is far warmer outside than it is in here."

"Yes, do. Go on back to your husbands. To your *happy* lives."

Poppy had turned but now swung her head back toward him. Bianca did the same. They both studied him a moment before linking arms and departing the drawing room.

"Why do I wonder when we'll see him again?" Poppy asked.

"Because it may be a very, very long time," Bianca said darkly.

Poppy feared she was right.

CHAPTER 9

*A*fter bidding farewell to Truro—and apologizing for failing to make any progress with the duke—Poppy and Bianca climbed into the Buckleigh coach and started toward Hartwell House. Unfortunately, they would not have good news to share. Poppy wanted to go back inside and throttle her brother.

"Now you're the one who looks as though she wants to commit murder," Bianca said. When Poppy looked at her in alarm, Bianca laughed. "You accused me of that the day you came to take me to Thornaby's house party."

Poppy relaxed against the squab. "So I did. Well, now I understand." She understood many things, including the effect of Felicity Garland.

"I think Felicity must have something to do with his change," Bianca mused, tapping her finger against the side of the coach.

"I was just thinking the same thing. Do you suppose she would tell us if we asked?"

"It's worth trying," Bianca said. "In the meantime, we must come to accept that our brother may be gone."

"I'm not ready to give up on him." Poppy

couldn't believe she was saying that. However, since she couldn't have children of her own, she was aware of how small their family was. They needed to be there for each other, even when one of them was, to quote Gabriel, a miserable pig.

They arrived at Hartwell House and carried in the baskets of treats from both the Buckleigh and Darlington kitchens. Mrs. Armstrong greeted them and ushered them into the drawing room, where the children were gathered for their afternoon story.

A small girl, perhaps five years old, named Susan ran to Bianca and threw her arms around her legs. "Lady Bianca! Did you come to read to us?"

Bianca laughed. "Why, yes." She looked over at Mrs. Armstrong, who nodded.

Mrs. Armstrong glanced sideways at Poppy. "I never read to them when Lady Buckleigh is here. Why would they want me when they can have her ladyship?"

"Yes, Bianca is quite good at doing all the voices and imbuing her oration with excitement."

"This also allows me a chance to speak with you about Judith. And Dinah." Mrs. Armstrong led Poppy into the sitting room. "I'm so looking forward to having Judith back. Are you certain Dinah is well enough to be on her own?"

Poppy removed her cloak and hat, setting them on the edge of the settee. "I think so. Dinah has taken to motherhood quite naturally."

"That's what Judith said in her last letter. I'm delighted to hear it—shocked, but delighted. Judith also said Nicola is a darling babe."

"She is indeed," Poppy agreed, somewhat bracing herself should Mrs. Armstrong wish to discuss their shared inability to bear children.

Mrs. Armstrong took a seat near the hearth. "And you think she'll make a good teacher here?"

Poppy set her gloves on her cloak. "I do. I've spent a great deal of time with her over the past weeks, and I like her very much. Her transition since giving birth has been nothing short of extraordinary. If her behavior with Nicola is any indication, she will be wonderful with the children. She was merely afraid. She didn't think she should be a mother."

"The poor dear. I shall like having her here—and the babe. I'm glad things have all worked out where she's concerned." Again, her gaze lingered on Poppy in such a way that Poppy anticipated she would say something about Dinah having a child while Poppy could not.

Hoping to avoid the topic, Poppy went to the fire to warm herself. "It's cold today."

"Yes, it's good of you to come out."

Relaxing, Poppy redirected the conversation. "We visited our brother in the hope of persuading him to reinstate his support of Hartwell House. I'm sorry to say we were not successful."

Mrs. Armstrong sighed. "I do appreciate you trying. We shall have to continue to make do. I learned long ago not to expect things."

A current of frustration whipped through Poppy. She pivoted toward Mrs. Armstrong. "It's not right. You should be able to expect support from the community, especially from those most in a position to help." Though Poppy had no knowledge of the Duke of Hartwell's accounts, she couldn't believe that Calder couldn't afford to help, nor could she believe their father had mismanaged anything.

"Your outrage on our behalf is heartwarming."

The more she thought about her brother's

unaccountable stinginess, the angrier she became. "My father would not be pleased. I don't
understand Calder. He didn't display even a bit
of remorse." Poppy began to pace, just a few
steps, back and forth in front of the fireplace.
"When I think of him alone in that huge house
while your rooms are leaking and you have
barely enough beds—not enough when Dinah
comes."

A wave of light-headedness washed over Poppy.
Her legs wobbled, and she had to grab the mantel
for support.

Mrs. Armstrong was beside her in a trice, her
arm clasping around Poppy's waist. "Here, sit
down." She guided Poppy to the settee. "Are you all
right?"

"Just a bit dizzy." A flush rose up Poppy's neck.
"And perhaps overheated. I think I was too close to
the fire."

Placing a hand on Poppy's forehead, Mrs. Armstrong pressed her lips together. "You don't feel too
warm. Should you lie down?"

"I think I'm fine." The dizziness returned along
with a surge of nausea. Poppy slapped her hand
over her mouth and closed her eyes, leaning back
against the settee.

"Oh dear, I'll be right back." Mrs. Armstrong
bustled toward the door.

"Would you mind bringing a few biscuits or
cakes?"

"You want to eat?" Mrs. Armstrong asked in
surprise.

"A nibble, perhaps." She'd felt unsettled like this
yesterday and the day before, and a few bites of a
biscuit had set her to rights.

Poppy closed her eyes as she waited for Mrs.
Armstrong to return. After a few minutes, the

sound of the woman's shoes on the floorboards drew Poppy's eyes open.

"Here." Mrs. Armstrong placed a cold cloth on Poppy's brow. "This should help. And here's a Banbury cake." She handed Poppy a small triangular cake dotted with currants.

Taking a bite, Poppy chewed slowly then took another bite. After four nibbles, she set the cake on the plate Mrs. Armstrong had placed on the table next to the settee. "Thank you, that's better."

Mrs. Armstrong sat back in her chair, her gaze never leaving Poppy. "How long have you been feeling like this?"

"A few days, but the sensation is mostly fleeting, occurring in the afternoon for a short while. I haven't been sleeping particularly well." Because of Gabriel. He wasn't sleeping in their bed, and she knew he was suffering.

"That must be it, then." Mrs. Armstrong sounded almost…disappointed. She turned her gaze to the fire.

"Did you suspect something else?"

"It was silly, and I shouldn't mention it." She slid Poppy a nervous glance. "It's just that…as soon as you arrived, you seemed different. I didn't want to think anything of it, but then after this…" She waved her hand. "Please pardon me."

Alarm pricked at Poppy's neck. She sat straight, taking the cloth from her forehead, then leaned toward Mrs. Armstrong. "Should I be worried?"

"I don't think so, but it can't be. I mean, it could, I suppose…"

Now Poppy was beginning to grow frustrated, and with that came another wave of nausea. She pressed the cloth to her cheeks.

Mrs. Armstrong's eyes sparked with concern. "Are you feeling ill again?"

"A bit. If you have information that would help me avoid this, I would appreciate you sharing it."

"Forgive my audacity, but when did you last have your courses?"

Thinking back, Poppy counted. The illness faded from her belly, and a strange tingling spread through her limbs. The room became a bit fuzzy, then snapped into sharp focus. "Too long ago," she whispered. She'd counted and tracked her bleeding for well over a year now. Her cycle was always the same. *Always.*

Until now.

Mrs. Armstrong moved to the settee next to Poppy, taking her hand. "Do you feel different in other ways? Tired? A tenderness in your breasts?"

Yes, but again, she'd attributed that to Gabriel. She was tired because she wasn't sleeping well. And her breasts ached a bit because she missed him touching them. But that was absurd, she now realized.

She was, after all this time, with child. She knew it as clearly as she knew Mrs. Armstrong was sitting beside her.

Poppy lowered the cloth to her lap, careless that it was making her skirt damp. "What do I do?"

"Rejoice." Mrs. Armstrong grinned, then wrapped her arms around Poppy in a fierce hug.

Hugging her back, Poppy began to laugh. Then Mrs. Armstrong joined in. Soon they were fighting to draw breath and dabbing at their eyes.

"Lord Darlington is going to be thrilled," Mrs. Armstrong said, beaming.

Poppy couldn't wait to tell him. This would draw him from his melancholy, and they could look to the future together.

The future. The birth of their child.

Gabriel would be terrified.

She thought of how Nicola's birth had affected him, the memories it had coaxed forth, the damage those had done. "I don't know how to tell him," she whispered, feeling his fear as if it were her own.

Mrs. Armstrong blinked in surprise. "Why?"

"He's...afraid. His mother died after giving birth. As did his sister."

"As did your mother." Mrs. Armstrong nodded. "Obviously, you will have to tell him." Her tone was wry but caring.

Poppy wondered if she could wait until she *had* to, until her condition became evident. She didn't want to worry him, especially if she wasn't truly pregnant. Or worse—if something happened and she didn't stay pregnant.

Now his fear *was* her fear. She couldn't tell him.

And yet, when she thought of how he'd kept Dinah from her for fear of causing her pain, she knew there could be no secrets between them. Pain and fear and loss and grief, they were part of life and they'd promised to share them with each other, to face and fight them together.

Poppy nodded at Mrs. Armstrong. "I'll tell him. Soon." In the meantime, she would confide in Bianca, who would be thrilled. Poppy prayed everything would turn out right.

Mrs. Armstrong gave her an encouraging smile. "You've been through so much. You deserve this happiness."

While that might be true, Poppy couldn't help but think Mrs. Armstrong had deserved it too, but hadn't been so fortunate.

Yes, there was pain and disappointment, but there was also love and acceptance. She looked around at the magnificent home Mrs. Armstrong—and her husband—had built, and she knew no matter what happened, she would be fine. No, she would be wonderful.

Life was a gift, and she would be eternally grateful for it.

~

*B*rooding had never been Gabriel's strong suit, and yet of late, he felt as if he could win a prize for gloominess. He stared into the fire, a glass of brandy dangling from his fingertips.

Poppy was home after spending last night at her sister's. He'd been disappointed when she hadn't returned after visiting Hartwood and Hartwell House, but could he blame her? He wasn't exactly good company. In truth, he oughtn't be surprised if she never came back.

But she had.

Grumbling, he lifted his glass only to find it was empty. *Hell.*

Pushing up from the chair, he went to the table next to the bed in the chamber he'd moved into a week ago. After Dinah had given birth to Nicola, simultaneously raising his worst demons and killing his last hope.

Was it any wonder he'd spent the past week in a stupor?

And how much longer do you plan to continue?

The voice in his head sounded like Poppy. He snorted as he reached for the bottle only to find it was empty. *Bloody hell.*

He set the glass down with a clack and crossed the room. Opening the door, he sucked in a breath at the sight of his wife standing over the threshold.

She wore a red velvet dressing gown that hugged her curves and outlined them to perfection. Her dark hair was gathered into a loose plait that hung over her right shoulder, the end of it curling against the swell of her breast. He wanted to tease her nipple with the silken strands. The erotic thought brought his cock to a half stand.

"May I came in?" She gave him a tentative look that made him feel like a beast.

He moved to the side, and she slowly walked in. He held the door as he watched her backside sway beneath the rich fabric. Mouth watering, he closed the door.

He was worse than a beast. Lusting after his wife when he wasn't even worthy of her.

She turned to face him, her chin high. "When are you returning to our bed?"

He blinked. She meant to cut right to it, then.

"Soon." What the hell did that mean?

She tipped her head to the side. "Why did you leave it in the first place?"

"You know why." The words were little more than grunts. The kind a beast would make.

"If I knew why, I wouldn't have asked." She gave him a perturbed stare and crossed her arms over her chest. "I know you're upset about what you re-membered. And probably about not being able to raise Nicola as our own. I'm upset about those things too." She moved toward him, and he tensed. He'd successfully avoided thinking too long about either of those things. The brandy had helped.

"I'm deeply troubled," she continued, her body swaying toward him and not stopping until she nearly touched his chest. "And I don't want to be troubled alone."

"Poppy." He said her name haltingly as he fought to keep hold on his equilibrium—and his sanity. "I can't do this."

She arched a brow at him. "I demand you do. You are my husband. You promised to be with me in sickness and in health, in good and bad. We are in this *together*."

Emotion roiled inside him—he gave in to the easy one: anger. "You didn't want to share your grief with me. Weeks you moped around here without talking to me. We weren't *together* then."

She flinched, and he felt horrid. "No, we weren't. I wish I had talked to you. Talk to me, Gabriel. Tell me what you're feeling."

"No." The denial squeezed past the rock in his throat.

"Then tell me something else. Tell me you miss me. You love me. You want me."

"All of those things," he rasped, his fingers itching to touch her, to claim her.

"Show me."

She'd said that to him weeks ago when he'd finally broken through her grief. Neatly, she'd turned the tables on him. God, he loved her.

He clasped her back and brought her roughly against his chest. His gaze held hers, riveted on the way her dark pupils enlarged into the blue-gray irises as her arousal grew.

"I've missed you." He reached between them and plucked at the clasps holding the gown closed.

The fabric fell open, and his mouth went dry. Her curves were so discernible because she wore nothing beneath the scarlet gown. "I love you."

He pushed the garment from her shoulders, sliding it down her arms, as he drank in her loveliness. From the column of her neck to the generous swell of her breast to the dip of her waist to the flare of her hip, he was entranced.

Picking up her plait between his thumb and forefinger, he dragged the end across her bare nipple. It rose to a stiff peak as she moaned, casting her head back and closing her eyes.

His cock raged with need, his body coursed with desire, his mind raced with passion. "I want you."

Her eyes came open, and she took his free hand. "Then take me."

She led him to the bed, where she climbed on top of the mattress and spread herself before him like a sumptuous buffet. There were too many delectable courses. He didn't know where to begin.

He still held her hair. Watching her, he swirled the end of the plait around her nipple, going in wider circles with each rotation. She came up off the bed, arching for more. He leaned down and kissed her other breast, his lips and tongue laving and sucking her flesh.

Then he abandoned her hair and cupped her breast, taking her in his hand and squeezing as he drew her other nipple into his mouth. Her cries grew louder. He gave her more, tugging on her and sucking hard.

She gasped, her hand clasping his neck. "Softer."

He lightened his touch—hands, fingers, mouth. Gently, he cupped both breasts and skimmed his thumbs across the nipples. She cried out his name and dug her fingers into his scalp.

There was something…off. She felt different, and she was behaving slightly…different. Her breasts felt heavier, almost larger, and she was so sensitive. Almost too sensitive…

He stilled. "Poppy, are you all right?"

She blinked her eyes open, taking a moment to focus on him. "Yes."

"Are you certain? Your breasts are different."

Her eyes widened. "You can tell?"

"Tell what?"

She hesitated, and panic began to bloom in his chest. "They *are* different. Because I'm with child."

The room went sideways. Gabriel reached for something and found the post of the bed. Clasping it tightly, he waited for the world to right itself. Only it couldn't.

She was pregnant.

The day he'd feared, the day he'd been relieved would never come, had arrived. He was going to lose her.

She sat up on the bed and put her hands on his waist, holding him tight. "Gabriel, it's going to be all right."

He shook his head. "You can't know that. How…"

"I think you know how." Her mouth curled into a smile, and all he could think was *How can you smile right now?*

"But why, after all this time?"

She shrugged. "I don't know. And I know you're scared. I am too. I'm also thrilled. Gabriel, this is a gift—"

How was losing her a gift? It was the exact opposite. He backed away from the bed. She made to follow him.

"Don't." He shook his head. "I can't. You can't be… No."

There would be no happy ending. Just misery and grief. And an empty, gaping hole before him where his beloved wife had been.

Gabriel turned and fled.

CHAPTER 10

$\mathcal{A}$fter dozing—to call it sleeping would be generous—on the small settee in his study, Gabriel had taken a ride around the estate. Then he'd gone into the town of Darlington. Now he was back on the estate, having wandered the day nearly away. He squinted up at the sky where the sun had just moved behind a high cloud on its way toward the horizon in just a couple of short hours. The day was cold and breezy, but he felt nothing inside or out.

Not that he *hadn't* felt something.

Last night's revelation, that Poppy was going to bear their child, still ricocheted through him. However, after spending most of the night pacing, tossing, and pacing again, he'd come to a sort of numb acceptance. After all, there was nothing he could do about the situation. She was pregnant, and her life was now at risk.

He blinked, realizing he'd found his way to Dinah's cottage. A figure walked about the front yard, and he recognized her—because she carried her babe.

What the hell was she doing?

Fury and fear unraveled within him, banishing

the numbness. He rode to the yard and dismounted, letting his horse graze. Then he stalked toward Dinah, who lifted her head toward him.

"What in God's name are you about?" he growled. "You and the babe shouldn't be out here. You'll catch your death of cold." He moved toward her, but she took a step back, her eyes narrowing.

"We won't either. I only just came out, and we won't stay long." She pursed her lips at him. "I needed a bit of exercise, if it's any of your concern."

He could barely see Nicola's head amidst the mass of blankets swaddling her, and he supposed she was warm enough. Still, why invite illness? "You must take better care."

"I beg your pardon, my lord, but did you stop just to lecture me?" she asked.

"No." Maybe? He hadn't really intended to come here, and yet here he was. Then he'd seen her outside with the babe and…lost what little composure he'd possessed.

"I notice you haven't visited at all since Nicola was born." She squinted up at him. "You don't like babies?"

He didn't know any babies. Why would he? "I've been busy."

"You weren't busy before she was born." She took a deep breath, and her gaze warmed with sympathy. "I know you and Lady Darlington hoped to raise her. I know you don't have children of your own, and given how long you've been married, it seems unlikely you will."

Gabriel wanted to laugh, but he feared he would cry instead. "As it happens, Lady Darlington is expecting." Why had he told her that?

Dinah's entire face lit up with joy. "How wonderful!" Then she immediately frowned. "Why has she been upset, then?"

"What do you mean?" Gabriel asked, though he suspected he knew.

"Every time she's visited since Nicola was born, I sense she's unsettled. Something is bothering her quite profoundly." She studied him intently. "Are you not aware?"

"I'm aware." He exhaled. "It's my fault."

Dinah blinked at him, her lips twisting into a frown. "Then why don't you fix things? Lady Darlington is one of the kindest, loveliest people I've ever met."

"It's rather, er, complicated."

"How can that be? If you say her upset is caused by you, uncause it." The babe stirred in her arms, and Dinah adjusted her hold. "You're both so lucky to have each other. What I wouldn't give to have a husband to help me. To support me. To love me."

Her words were a series of arrows piercing through his fear and anxiety. Yes, they were lucky. To have each other. And now to have a child coming. God, he was already so in love with him or her, and it would be months and months until he met the child. He just prayed he would get the chance.

"I'm terrified," he whispered.

"Could you be more terrified than a young woman who was attacked by her employer, cast out by him and then her family, and who, without the kindness of strangers, would have birthed her babe in a filthy workhouse or worse?" She made it seem as if he shouldn't be frightened, but his fear was real and paralyzing.

"You're a brave young woman," he said quietly. "I am a man who expects to lose his wife and likely his child after she gives birth. Tell me, how do I live with that apprehension every day?"

"You do because the alternative is that you don't live at all. When I said I would give anything to have what you do, I would take it if even for a short while. Any time is better than none." She stepped closer to him as the baby began to make soft noises. "Lady Darlington may die, but the odds are against it. Only you can decide if you want to cower in fear or walk straight into the future with courage and purpose. I had no choice, and right now, I can see that was a good thing."

She was right. He had a choice. He had the luxury of being a self-centered lout. A wave of disgust washed over him.

"What will you choose? Fear or joy?" Nicola began to cry, and Dinah excused herself before walking back into the cottage.

Fear or joy…

Gabriel conjured an image of Poppy's belly swelling, of her laughing in the summertime as she stroked the roundness of her midsection. Her dream had come true, and he realized his had too —to see her happy.

There was no choice to make, not when Poppy was the base of everything he was and everything he wanted to be. Gabriel strode to his horse and quickly mounted. He raced back to the stables and dashed into the house in search of his wife.

"She's already left for the assembly, my lord. Lord and Lady Buckleigh came and conveyed her to Hartwell."

Bloody, bloody hell. "Walker, I'll need a bath." Gabriel ran upstairs, intent on the fastest toilet of his life. He had to pursue his wife.

And joy.

～

*T*he assembly dripped with pine boughs and ribbon. Lanterns flickered, and mistletoe hung in the corners. Arrack punch, like the kind they served at Vauxhall in London, graced the refreshment table, as did a variety of sweet confections. A huge blancmange in the shape of a Yule log and decorated with pine sat in the center.

The scene should have filled Poppy with cheerful expectation. But without Gabriel at her side, she felt sad. Particularly since this assembly was where they'd met three years before. Being here without him didn't feel right. In fact, she'd almost decided not to come, but Bianca and Ash had already been en route to fetch her, and she didn't want them to have gone out of their way for nothing.

So she'd pretended to be happy and made up a story about Gabriel being ill.

"There's Felicity," Bianca whispered, inclining her head toward a tall blonde woman garbed in a blue gown.

Poppy picked Felicity out of the crowd. "Should we go and speak with her?"

"Of course." Bianca took Ash's arm, and the three of them crossed the assembly room to where Felicity stood with her mother. Mrs. Templeton looked a bit frail. She clung to her daughter's arm.

"Come, Mama. You must sit. Otherwise, I will rethink my decision to allow you to come. You are still recovering."

"Oh, pooh. I'm fine, dear. But yes, a chair would not come amiss." Mrs. Templeton smiled up at her daughter and the change in her expression made her look much more robust, if that were possible.

Felicity saw them then, her green eyes lighting

with recognition. "Good evening, Lady Darlington and Lady... Buckleigh, is it?"

"Yes," Bianca answered. "Allow me to present my husband, the Earl of Buckleigh. Ash, this is Mrs. Felicity Garland."

Ash inclined his head. "Of course I remember you, Mrs. Garland."

Felicity rose from her curtsey with wide eyes. "Ash, as in little Ashton Rutledge? I would not have recognized you."

"None of us did," Bianca said with a laugh.

"How marvelous to see you all." Felicity glanced around. "Where is your brother? I've yet to encounter him since I returned to Hartwell."

Poppy and Bianca exchanged a wary look. "I doubt he'll be here this evening," Poppy said smoothly. "He's not very social these days. The dukedom keeps him quite busy."

"That's too bad," Felicity said. "I'd looked forward to seeing him. I suppose I'll just have to pay a call."

Bianca's gaze snapped to Poppy, and she opened her mouth. Poppy worried that nothing helpful would come out, so she rushed to say, "Perhaps send him a note asking when he receives visitors." She added a placid smile.

Ash sucked in a breath, his eyes fixed on the entrance. "He's here."

All four women turned their heads to see Calder standing just inside the threshold. Indeed, a hush fell over the entire assembly.

Calder surveyed the large room, his gaze moving quickly until settling on them. No, not on them. On Felicity Garland. He strode toward their group, and the crowd magically parted as if he were an ancient river carving its way through a hillside.

"Good evening," he announced as he arrived, standing next to Poppy.

"Good evening," Poppy said, eyeing him with disbelief. He was garbed in unforgiving black save his white shirt and cravat. Gentlemen typically dressed up their assembly attire with something festive. Calder did not.

Felicity curtsied and helped her mother do the same. "Your Grace, I was just telling your sisters how I looked forward to seeing you."

"Did you? How surprising after all this time." Calder's voice carried an edge—not the same obnoxious tone he'd had of late. This was something different, something that cut far deeper.

"Yes, it's been many years," Felicity said. "I do hope we'll find time to visit. If you'll excuse me, I need to see my mother to a chair."

It was a perfect invitation for Calder to step forward and offer to help. Given how he'd immediately spotted Felicity and walked straight to her, Poppy would have expected him to provide assistance. Instead, he stood there, his gaze cold as he regarded her mother.

"Allow me to help," Ash said, presenting his arm. He sent a glance toward Calder as Mrs. Templeton accepted his assistance.

"Thank you, Lord Buckleigh."

"I'll be right there, Mama," Felicity said. She watched as they walked away, then looked to Calder.

"Why are you here?" he asked sharply, his voice low so that only the four of them could hear.

Poppy suddenly felt as though she and Bianca were intruding. She edged close to her sister and grazed her elbow against Bianca's arm.

Felicity drew back, her features tightening with confusion. "Everyone comes to the assembly."

Not everyone. Poppy was painfully aware of her husband's absence, particularly now that Calder of all people was here.

"Not here at the assembly, here in *Hartwell*." There was an accusatory note to his statement. Poppy tensed.

"My mother returned last year, and several weeks ago, she became ill. I came to take care of her."

"So your visit is temporary."

She narrowed one eye at him very briefly. "I haven't yet decided." Casting a smile toward Poppy and Bianca, who'd linked arms, Felicity continued, "I'm especially glad to be here for the holidays. No one celebrates better than the people of Hartwell. I am so looking forward to St. Stephen's Day, but I was sad to hear Hartwood would not be hosting the event. I'd feared you were ill." She regarded Calder closely as if she could discern some sort of malady.

Would that she could, for there was absolutely something wrong with him. This was not their brother!

"I am not, as you can see."

"You don't appear to be, and yet you aren't quite the man I remember." Felicity shook her head. "But then it's been over a decade."

"Yes, people change over time. And some people change overnight." Calder gave Felicity a haughty stare. "I'm not sure the woman I remember ever existed."

Oh dear, this was not the place to have such a conversation. Poppy moved toward her brother, reaching for his arm. "Calder, perhaps we should—"

He swung his gaze toward her, glowering. "Don't touch me. I will say what I like."

"Not to my wife, you won't." Gabriel inserted himself between Calder and Poppy. She stared at him, shocked he was there. She'd been so intent on her brother that she hadn't noticed his entry. Glancing about, she realized the entire assembly was focused on Calder.

"Calder, you're causing a scene," Poppy whispered.

Calder's gaze darkened, and his lip curled. Before he could speak, Gabriel edged toward him. "Careful, Chill, don't let this scene escalate into something else."

Calder glared at all of them, but his most hateful stare went to Felicity. "I've come to see what I needed to. And now I am free." He spun on his heel and stalked from the assembly.

Bianca smiled broadly and looked urgently at Poppy and Ash, her eyes asking them to join her in appearing pleasant. As if their brother hadn't just behaved like a horrendous boor in the middle of the holiday assembly.

Except Poppy couldn't quite bring herself to do anything but stare at her husband. He was here.

Gabriel turned to her. "I didn't mean to drive him away."

"It was for the best," she said.

He offered her his arm. "Shall we take a turn?"

She ought to introduce Felicity and ensure the situation was truly settled, but she was too wrapped up in wanting to know why Gabriel had come. Wordlessly, she put her hand on his sleeve, and he led her to the periphery, where they began a promenade around the hall.

He spoke first. "I'm sorry. That I wasn't at home when you left for the assembly. That I've been distant and self-absorbed. That I reacted like an idiot when you told me about the babe."

Her heart leapt, and she squeezed his arm. He steered her into a corner, well away from anyone else.

She turned toward him, standing close, her eyes searching his face. "You were scared."

"There is no past tense." His tone was dry, and she was so grateful for even a modicum of humor. "I am terrified, but I am also overjoyed. I realized I prefer the latter, so I'm going to focus on that."

"You 'realized'?"

"I might have had some help from Dinah. Perspective is a powerful thing."

"It is." She rested her palm on his lapel. "So is sadness and fear. I know what that feels like," she said softly.

"Of course you do, my love. We are on this journey together—for better or worse. I think we are both due for some of the better." His mouth ticked up, and her heart somersaulted.

"I think so too. I promise I won't die. And neither will the babe." She touched her other hand to her stomach.

His smile took on a sad tinge, but only for a moment. "You can't promise that. However, I believe everything will work out as it should, and I plan to spend every day basking in the love we share and the joy of thinking about tomorrow."

"Even if that tomorrow doesn't come?" She almost wished she hadn't asked that. He'd come so far already.

"But it will, whether we want it to or not, whether we are here or not. So why not plan for the best?" He winked at her. "I'm still working on this, so bear with me."

She grinned up at him. "As you said, it's a journey. I will be with you every step of the way."

The first strains of music started. "Speaking of

steps," Gabriel said. "I believe it's time for you to dance with me."

A laugh bubbled up from deep inside her. "That's what you said to me three years ago—you didn't really ask. I thought you were so arrogant."

"It was all bluster."

"It worked."

"If I'm correct, there was also a bit of mistletoe involved." He waggled his brows at her.

She glanced up. "Look."

Hanging above them was a bouquet of mistletoe.

"I didn't kiss you three years ago."

"You couldn't. And you shouldn't now."

"Hmm, this seems like a question of perspective. For me, I have no problem kissing you here."

She giggled. "Then who am I to quarrel?"

He bent down and brushed his lips over hers. "Consider that a prologue to the story I'll tell you later. Now, let us dance."

As Gabriel swept her into his arms on the dance floor, an encompassing joy washed over her. This was a holiday season she would never forget.

EPILOGUE

August 1812

*P*oppy's anguished cries filled the chamber. Gabriel had weighed whether to be present for the birth, and now he was beginning to question his decision.

"There's the head!" Dr. Fisk called.

Mrs. Fisk looked up at Poppy with warm encouragement. "One more push now, love."

Red-faced, Poppy bore down. She squeezed Gabriel's hand so hard, he feared it would never have blood flowing through it again.

But he'd give up anything for her, including his hand.

"Please let her be all right, please, please, please." The silent plea played over and over in his mind, a chorus of hope.

A loud squall filled the chamber. Poppy exhaled loudly, and her grip on his hand finally loosened.

"We have an heir," Dr. Fisk said, grinning. He glanced over at Gabriel as he handed the babe to

Mrs. Fisk. She did something with him, but Gabriel's attention was entirely focused on the exhausted but beaming face of his wife.

She looked up at him. "Did you hear that? You have a son."

"*We* have a son." He was glad his voice didn't sound as shaky as he felt. He lifted her hand and kissed the back before tucking it against her side. Leaning down, he kissed her dewy forehead. "As long as I live, I will never do anything as miraculous or spectacular as you did today."

She laughed. "I can't say I disagree with you."

Mrs. Fisk appeared at his side. "My lord, may I present your son." She handed him the swaddled babe, his pink face scrunched and crying. "I do think he may be hungry." She turned to attend Poppy, but Gabriel was now entirely focused on his son.

He touched the boy's tiny button nose. His cries faded, and his eyes opened. They were blue with a bit of gray—like his mother's, though he'd heard they might not stay that way. He decided they would. Of course they would.

Love, fierce and all-encompassing, assaulted Gabriel, nearly stealing his breath. He'd loved this child for months, but this was different—richer and more complete. He now understood how Dinah had completely changed her mind the moment she'd held Nicola.

"Her ladyship is ready for him." Mrs. Fisk took the babe and put him into Poppy's arms. Mrs. Fisk had arranged her so that her breast was exposed and began to show her how to nurse their son. It was the most beautiful thing Gabriel had ever seen.

Enchanted, he watched tears track down Poppy's face, her smile soft and adoring as she cradled their son. She stroked his cheek and whispered words of love. Words that echoed deep in Gabriel's heart. He wiped a hand over his wet eyes, grinning.

A few moments later, he realized they were alone in their bedchamber—just the three of them. He could scarcely believe it.

"Thaddeus, I think," she said, her gaze locking with Gabriel's. They'd discussed several names that meant gift, for that's what this child was.

Gabriel thought of the other names they'd considered but agreed he looked like Thaddeus. "Yes."

A while later, Thaddeus dozed upon his mother's breast, and Gabriel sat, weary but content, in a chair beside the bed. He was fairly certain Poppy was asleep, her eyes closed, her breaths deep and even. All was well. For now.

Stop it.

He refused to worry or be afraid. The birth had gone exceptionally well according to Dr. Fisk. Even so, he'd agreed to stay with them for three days to alleviate Gabriel's concern.

"I know I can't protect you from everything, but I will do my best," he whispered, gazing at his beloved wife and son. "Always."

Her eyes fluttered open, and her mouth curved into a smile. "I know you will. And we'll be right here doing the same for you."

"I made something," he said, his pulse quickening with anticipation. "I'll be right back."

He went into the sitting room and found what he sought—one of the footmen had brought it up earlier in the day. Hefting the piece of furniture, he carried it into the bedchamber and set it next to the bed.

Poppy gasped when she saw the cradle. "It's beautiful. When I asked if you planned to make something, you said you would…later. I thought you were afraid," she said softly.

"I was, but I told you I wasn't going to surrender to fear." He'd crafted the piece with love and hope. Made of oak, he'd carved greenery and mistletoe into the wood.

"It reminds me of Christmas," she said, smiling.

"The season of joy and hope." Gabriel leaned down and kissed her, his lips lingering softly against hers. The future stretched before them—bright and long. A peace settled over him.

"Thank you, my love," she whispered. "This is the most perfect gift."

He shook his head in gentle disagreement, love coursing through him. "No, that would be you and our son."

Find out what happens with the St. Stephen's Day party and why Calder is such a Scrooge in Joy to the Duke! Coming November 12, 2019!

Thank you so much for reading The Gift of the Marquess! It's the second book in my Regency holiday series, Love is All Around. I hope you enjoyed it! Don't miss the final book in the trilogy, Joy to the Duke!

Would you like to know when my next book is available and to hear about sales and deals? Sign up for my VIP newsletter at https://www.darcyburke. com/readergroup, follow me on social media:

Facebook: https://facebook.com/DarcyBurkeFans
Twitter at @darcyburke

Instagram at darcyburkeauthor
Pinterest at darcyburkewrite

And follow me on Bookbub to receive updates on pre-orders, new releases, and deals!

Need more Regency romance? Check out my other historical series:

The Spitfire Society - Meet the smart, independent women who've decided they don't need Society's rules, their families' expectations, or, most importantly, a husband. But just because they don't need a man doesn't mean they might not *want* one…

The Untouchables - Swoon over twelve of Society's most eligible and elusive bachelor peers and the bluestockings, wallflowers, and outcasts who bring them to their knees!

Wicked Dukes Club - six books written by me and my BFF, NYT Bestselling Author Erica Ridley. Meet the unforgettable men of London's most notorious tavern, The Wicked Duke. Seductively handsome, with charm and wit to spare, one night with these rakes and rogues will never be enough...

Secrets and Scandals - six epic stories set in London's glittering ballrooms and England's lush countryside, and the first one, Her Wicked Ways, is free!

Legendary Rogues - Four intrepid heroines and adventurous heroes embark on exciting quests across Regency England and Wales!
If you like contemporary romance, I hope you'll

check out my Ribbon Ridge series available from
Avon Impulse, and the continuation of Ribbon
Ridge in So Hot.

I hope you'll consider leaving a review at your
favorite online vendor or networking site!

I appreciate my readers so much. Thank you, thank
you, *thank you*.

AUTHOR'S NOTE

One day last spring I thought it would be fun to write a Christmas trilogy and base the stories on classic holiday tales. The Gift of the Magi by O. Henry is a lovely story and served as the inspiration for The Gift of the Marquess. This was my first foray into writing a romance where the hero and heroine had already fallen in love and were married. As someone who's been married for nearly twenty-eight years (as of this writing), I can attest to the fact that marriage does not end the conflict—or the romance! It was very rewarding to write Poppy and Gabriel's moving journey.

The Institution for Impoverished Women is something entirely of my own creation. It's based on workhouses of the time, but I didn't want a "real" workhouse which separated men and women (and children—they didn't see their parents often) and was typically more like a prison.

Thank you Julie Kenner for the countless phone calls it took to get this just right.

I hope you enjoyed this inspired story! And Merry Christmas. :)

When We Kiss
You're Still the One

Ribbon Ridge: So Hot

So Good
So Right
So Wrong

The Untouchables Series

THE FORBIDDEN DUKE

"I LOVED this story!!" 5 Stars

-Historical Romance Lover

"This is a wonderful read and I can't wait to see what comes next in this amazing series..." 5 Stars

-Teatime and Books

THE DUKE of DARING

"You will not be able to put it down once you start. Such a good read."

-Books Need TLC

"An unconventional beauty set on life as a spinster meets the one man who might change her mind, only to find his painful past makes it impossible to love. A wonderfully emotional journey from attraction, to friendship, to a love that conquers all."

-Bronwen Evans, *USA Today* Bestselling Author

THE DUKE of DECEPTION

"...an enjoyable, well-paced story ... Ned and Aquilla are an engaging, well-matched couple –

strong, caring and compassionate; and ...it's easy to believe that they will continue to be happy together long after the book is ended."

-All About Romance

"This is my favorite so far in the series! They had chemistry from the moment they met...their passion leaps off the pages."

-Sassy Book Lover

THE DUKE of DESIRE

"Masterfully written with great characterization...with a flourish toward characters, secrets, and romance... Must read addition to "The Untouchables" series!"

-My Book Addiction and More

"If you are looking for a truly endearing story about two people who take the path least travelled to find the other, with a side of 'YAH THAT'S HOT!' then this book is absolutely for you!"

-The Reading Café

THE DUKE of DEFIANCE

"This story was so beautifully written, and it hooked me from page one. I couldn't put the book down and just had to read it in one sitting even though it meant reading into the wee hours of the morning."

-Buried Under Romance

"I loved the Duke of Defiance! This is the kind of book you hate when it is over and I had to make myself stop reading just so I wouldn't have to leave the fun of Knighton's (aka Bran) and Joanna's story!"

-Behind Closed Doors Book Review

THE DUKE of DANGER

"The sparks fly between them right from the start... the HEA is certainly very hard-won, and well-deserved."

-All About Romance

"Another book hangover by Darcy! Every time I pick a favorite in this series, she tops it. The ending was perfect and made me want more."

-Sassy Book Lover

THE DUKE of ICE

"Each book gets better and better, and this novel was no exception. I think this one may be my fave yet! 5 out 5 for this reader!"

-Front Porch Romance

"An incredibly emotional story...I dare anyone to stop reading once the second half gets under way because this is intense!"

-Buried Under Romance

THE DUKE of RUIN

"This is a fast paced novel that held me until the last page."

" ...everything I could ask for in a historical romance... impossible to stop reading."

THE DUKE of LIES

"THE DUKE OF LIES is a work of genius! The characters are wonderfully complex, engaging; there is much mystery, and so many, many lies from so many people; I couldn't wait to see it all uncovered."

"..the epitome of romantic [with]...a bit of danger/action. The main characters are mature, fierce, passionate, and full of surprises. If you are a hopeless romantic and you love reading stories that'll leave you feeling like you're walking on clouds then you need to read this book or maybe even this entire series."

THE DUKE of SEDUCTION

"There were tears in my eyes for much of the last 10% of this book. So good!"

"An absolute joy to read... I always recommend Darcy!"

-Brittany and Elizabeth's Book Boutique

THE DUKE of KISSES

"Don't miss this magnificent read. It has some comedic fun, heartfelt relationships, heartbreaking moments, and horrifying danger."

-The Reading Café

"...my favorite story in the series. Fans of Regency romances will definitely enjoy this book."

-Two Ends of the Pen

THE DUKE of DISTRACTION

"Count on Burke to break a heart as only she can. This couple will get under the skin before they steal your heart."

-Hopeless Romantic

"Darcy Burke never disappoints. Her storytelling is just so magical and filled with passion. You will fall in love with the characters and the world she creates!"

-Teatime and Books

Secrets & Scandals Series

HER WICKED WAYS

"A bad girl heroine steals both the show and a highwayman's heart in Darcy Burke's deliciously wicked debut."

–Courtney Milan, *NYT* Bestselling Author

"…fast paced, very sexy, with engaging characters."

–*Smexybooks*

HIS WICKED HEART

"Intense and intriguing. Cinderella meets *Fight Club* in a historical romance packed with passion, action and secrets."

–Anna Campbell, *Seven Nights in a Rogue's Bed*

"A romance...to make you smile and sigh…a wonderful read!"

–*Rogues Under the Covers*

TO SEDUCE A SCOUNDREL

"Darcy Burke pulls no punches with this sexy, romantic page-turner. Sevrin and Philippa's story grabs you from the first scene and doesn't let go. *To Seduce a Scoundrel* is simply delicious!"

–Tessa Dare, *NYT* Bestselling Author

"I was captivated on the first page and didn't let go until this glorious book was finished!"

–*Romancing the Book*

TO LOVE A THIEF

"With refreshing circumstances surrounding both the hero and the heroine, a nice little mystery, and a touch of heat, this novella was a perfect way to pass the day."

–The Romanceaholic

"A refreshing read with a dash of danger and a little heat. For fans of honorable heroes and fun heroines who know what they want and take it."

-The Luv NV

NEVER LOVE A SCOUNDREL

"I loved the story of these two misfits thumbing their noses at society and finding love." Five stars.

–A Lust for Reading

"A nice mix of intrigue and passion...wonderfully complex characters, with flaws and quirks that will draw you in and steal your heart."

–BookTrib

SCOUNDREL EVER AFTER

"There is something so delicious about a bad boy, no matter what era he is from, and Ethan was definitely delicious."

-A Lust for Reading

"I loved the chemistry between the two main characters...Jagger/Ethan is not what he seems at all and neither is sweet society Miss Audrey. They are believably compatible."

-Confessions of a College Angel

Legendary Rogues Series

LADY of DESIRE

"A fast-paced mixture of adventure and romance, very much in the mould of *Romancing the Stone* or *Indiana Jones*."

-All About Romance

"...gave me such a book hangover! ...addictive...one of the most entertaining stories I've read this year!"

-Adria's Romance Reviews

ROMANCING the EARL

"Once again Darcy Burke takes an interesting story and...turns it into magic. An exceptionally well-written book."

-Bodice Rippers, Femme Fatale, and Fantasy

"...A fast paced story that was exciting and interesting. This is a definite must add to your book lists!"

-Kilts and Swords

LORD of FORTUNE

"I don't think I know enough superlatives to describe this book! It is wonderfully, magically delicious. It sucked me in from the very first sentence and didn't turn me loose—not even at the end ..."

"If you love a deep, passionate romance with a bit of mystery, then this is the book for you!"

CAPTIVATING the SCOUNDREL

"I am in absolute awe of this story. Gideon and Daphne stole all of my heart and then some. This book was such a delight to read."

"Darcy knows how to end a series with a bang! Daphne and Gideon are a mix of enemies and allies turned lovers that will have you on the edge of your seat at every turn."

Contemporary Romance

Ribbon Ridge Series

A contemporary family saga featuring the Archer family of sextuplets who return to their small Oregon wine country town to confront tragedy and find love...

The "multilayered plot keeps readers invested in the story line, and the explicit sensuality adds to the excitement that will have readers craving the next Ribbon Ridge offering."

-*Library Journal* Starred Review on YOURS
TO HOLD

"Darcy Burke writes a uniquely touching and heart-warming series about the love, pain, and joys of family as well as the love that feeds your soul when you meet "the one.""

-*The Many Faces of Romance*

I can't tell you how much I love this series. Each book gets better and better.

-*Romancing the Readers*

"Darcy Burke's Ribbon Ridge series is one of my all-time favorites. Fall in love with the Archer family, I know I did."

-*Forever Book Lover*

Ribbon Ridge: So Hot

SO GOOD

" ...worth the read with its well-written words, beautiful descriptions, and likeable characters...they are flirty, sexy and a match made in wine heaven."

-*Harlequin Junkie* Top Pick

"I absolutely love the characters in this book and

the families. I honestly could not put it down and
finished it in a day."

-*Chin Up Mom*

SO RIGHT

"This is another great story by Darcy Burke.
Painting pictures with her words that make you
want to sit and stare at them for hours. I love the
banter between the characters and the general
sense of fun and friendliness."

-*The Ardent Reader*

" ...the romance is emotional; the characters are
spirited and passionate... "

-*The Reading Café*

SO WRONG

"As usual, Ms. Burke brings you fun characters and
witty banter in this sweet hometown series. I loved
the dance between Crystal and Jamie as they
fought their attraction."

-*The Many Faces of Romance*

"I really love both this series and the Ribbon Ridge
series from Darcy Burke. She has this way of
taking your heart and ripping it right out of your
chest one second and then the next you are
laughing at something the characters are doing."

-*Romancing the Readers*

ABOUT THE AUTHOR

Darcy Burke is the USA Today Bestselling Author of sexy, emotional historical and contemporary romance. Darcy wrote her first book at age 11, a happily ever after about a swan addicted to magic and the female swan who loved him, with exceedingly poor illustrations. Join her Reader Club at https://www.darcyburke.com/readerclub.

A native Oregonian, Darcy lives on the edge of wine country with her guitar-strumming husband, their two hilarious kids who seem to have inherited the writing gene. They're a crazy cat family with two Bengal cats, a small, fame-seeking cat named after a fruit, and an older rescue Maine Coon who is the master of chill and five a.m. serenading. In her "spare" time Darcy is a serial volunteer enrolled in a 12-step program where one learns to say "no," but she keeps having to start over. Her happy places are Disneyland and Labor Day weekend at the Gorge. Visit Darcy online at https://www.darcyburke.com and follow her social media: Facebook at http://www.facebook.com/darcyburkefans, Twitter @darcyburke at https://www.twitter.com/darcyburke, Instagram at https://www.instagram/darcyburkeauthor, and Pinterest at https://www.pinterest.com/darcyburkewrite.